W9-BFC-068

QUEST FOR THE
NAUTILUS

YOUNG CAPTAIN NEMO
QUEST FOR THE NAUTILUS

JASON HENDERSON

FEIWEL AND FRIENDS
NEW YORK

A FEIWEL AND FRIENDS BOOK
An imprint of Macmillan Publishing Group, LLC
120 Broadway, New York, NY 10271

Printed in the United States of America by LSC Communications, Harrisonburg,
Virginia

Our books may be purchased in bulk for promotional, educational, or business use.
Please contact your local bookseller or the Macmillan Corporate and Premium Sales
Department at (800) 221-7945 ext. 5442 or by email at
MacmillanSpecialMarkets@macmillan.com.

Library of Congress Cataloging-in-Publication Data is available.
ISBN 978-1-250-17324-9 (hardcover) / ISBN 978-1-250-17325-6 (ebook)

Book design by Katie Klimowicz

Feiwel and Friends logo designed by Filomena Tuosto
First edition, 2020

1 3 5 7 9 10 8 6 4 2

mackids.com

For Sophia, who helped me rediscover heroes

QUEST FOR THE
NAUTILUS

PROLOGUE

SOMEWHERE BELOW THE NORTH PACIFIC

THREE MILES BELOW the ocean's surface, the earth is dark. Mountains rise and valleys spread out; billowing silt ripples over old bones and lost, crumpled wrecks. Sunlight may as well be a myth, and crawling beasts, colorless and dense, make their homes in a world where humans cannot survive.

Where humans cannot survive. Not without help, anyway.

The whirring servomechanisms in Dr. David Nemo's suit hummed in strange mechanical chords with his every step. David looked behind him toward his vehicle and saw another scientist walking toward him, clad like him in a hardened, mechanically assisted deep-dive suit that glistened silver against the backdrop of the silty floor.

David unclipped a tablet computer from his suit to

bring it up toward his faceplate. The whirring sound of the servos in his suit quieted as he turned, casting beams of light from the LEDs that lined his helmet. He almost didn't need the light just now. Several hundred yards away, a parked Nemotech rover rumbled, kicking up clouds of silt as brilliant floodlights on the rover's roof pointed in all directions and lit up the valley for three quarters of a mile.

"You want to give me a hand with this?" Dr. Sharmila Kassam was carrying a white, four-and-a-half-foot-tall metal barrel using a pair of silver handles on its sides. She held the barrel in front of her as she walked.

David studied a screen on the tablet and saw faint green images circling the map that represented the valley in which he stood. He didn't look up at Sharmila. "You seem to be handling it okay. The servos in your elbows should allow you to lift three hundred pounds without any effort on your part." He had designed the suits himself.

"Still hits my knees." Sharmila set the barrel down when she got near. "You have carried barrels, right?"

"Seriously, you could lift it over your head." He expanded the screen with the fingers of his glove. This time he looked up and smirked at Sharmila. "But thanks."

Sharmila nodded, her own smirk visible inside her faceplate. She rested her hand on the barrel's lid and looked up. "Do you see the Lodgers?"

"I can see a few on the scanner," David said. "About a dozen." The creatures they had taken to calling

Lodgers—for their habit of putting on and wearing giant, old wrecked planes—were still out of sight above them, circling the valley and possibly exploring beyond.

Sharmila flattened her gloved hand against the top of the barrel, and filaments along the palm and fingers glowed red as soon as they detected the scanner in the barrel lid. A metal panel slid away into the lid, revealing a glassy surface that Sharmila hovered her glowing palm over. A series of short bursts of light sparkled against her palm, and then the metal panel popped back into place. The cover of the barrel unhooked itself with a *clunk* that David could hear through the water, and Sharmila lifted the lid away.

The inside of the barrel gave off a slight glow, and though David couldn't feel it through his suit, he knew that removing the lid had also activated heating elements that would make the cargo nice and warm. The barrel was full to the brim with countless pellets of bright blue plastic, each about the size of a marble. The cargo was patterned after the pellets that occurred in the Great Pacific Garbage Patch in the middle of the Pacific Ocean, where bits of plastic debris and litter battered against one another and against waves until they formed small, rounded globs. The Lodgers had taken to treating the pellets of the Patch as their main food source, and these in the barrel were especially made by the Nemos to suit their tastes.

One of the shapes on the screen grew larger, and David looked up. The first creature to arrive dipped down toward the scientists and whipped its wings to slow its descent. The wings were silver and still painted with old American World War II markings. Inside the broken-glass cockpit, stalk eyes blinked and swayed in the water. Tendrils searched through crevices along the wings. This was one of the first Lodgers that the Nemos had ever seen, a creature like a crustacean that inhabited the body of a B-17 bomber.

David tapped a button on the tablet, and the barrel began to spew its contents in a column that rose forty feet up into the water and started to spread out, sparkling like a galaxy. The B-17 Lodger swam through, taking in pellets as it went.

David's tablet filled with more green shapes as the creatures emerged out of the darkness, some of them whipping wings of ancient airplanes, some gliding in suits of custom-crafted Nemotech armor. The armor was modular, allowing the strange creatures to experiment, if it could be called that, with fitting different sections to their particular needs. David took a moment to study them.

A thrumming rumble filled the water and made David's suit vibrate. The sound first came from the B-17 and then was followed by the others. The Lodgers were vocalizing. But so far it had been impossible to understand what, if anything, the vocalizations meant.

"What are you going to try today?" Sharmila asked.

David tabbed over to a new screen on the tablet and found a keyboard with a series of sliders. "Communication," he said. "They've responded to pulses before, but today I'm going to make up some grammar." The communication program had been created by Peter, who served on the Nemoship *Obscure* with David's son, Gabriel, and another of Gabriel's friends. If *served* was the right word for volunteers who were still in school.

Very likely the pulses it sent were gibberish to the Lodgers, if they had a language at all. But he felt certain that he *had* generated a response. "Any day now," he said, "I'm going to get one of them to say hi, and then—"

Whunk.

The sounds emanating from the rover stopped instantly with the crunch of metal. David turned, the servomechanisms in his suit singing out as he spun. At first he thought that one of the Lodgers must have become irritated by the sound coming from the rover, which would have been a really interesting development in itself. So far they had more or less ignored him, unless you counted the attention that the little submarine may or may not have just earned. But no, there was no Lodger chewing away at the rover.

Sharmila staggered in her suit, suddenly seeing the same thing he was. On the roof of the vehicle, not far from one of the floodlights, was a circular machine that at first reminded David of an old satellite. His next thought was: *It's a* spider.

The bulk of it, its main body, was a silver globe about three feet wide. Out of the globe protruded metal, multi-jointed legs and cables with pointed, metallic ends.

"That's…some kind of drone." Sharmila sounded as shocked as David felt.

David nodded as he started running toward the rover, the knee servos in his suit whirring as he and Sharmila moved quickly across the ocean floor.

"What is it doing?" David asked. He tapped a button on his helmet. "Nemolab, this is Dr. David. We've run into a strange drone." Nemolab was a large complex of domes about twenty miles away on the bottom of the ocean. It was a closely guarded secret, the most precious stronghold of the Nemo family.

"Or, rather, the drone has run into our rover," Sharmila said.

"That makes it sound like an accident." As he got closer, he could see that there was no way this was accidental. The drone shoved aside the battered loudspeaker on the roof of the rover and unfolded one of its arms as the pointed end began spinning. A few particles of Lodger food had floated there, and he could see them swirling in a mini tornado around the drone's hand.

The hand began to drill through the roof of the rover

as David drew an energy weapon from his shoulder. The device fired "pincer" energy, a sort of dense and focused plasma that could stun people and disrupt machinery. But whereas a pincer rifle could fire sustained streams of the stuff, his hand weapon fired only bolts. He had to stop and aim carefully, and when he pulled the trigger, the bolt sizzled from the barrel and flew wide, glancing off the roof of the rover and missing the drone entirely.

Sharmila fired hers, and her bolt hit the drone along the top, just barely. The energy arced and danced around the drone and dissipated in the water. The drone kept drilling.

"What's going on?" came the voice from the control room back at the lab.

"I don't know." Above him, the Lodgers fed on, satisfied in their own world. "This drone is drilling into the roof of our rover."

Suddenly the drilling stopped, and David saw silvery metal undulate in the arm of the drone. The arm was vibrating as the drone sat still.

David reached the rover and leapt up onto the hood of the vehicle. He fell through the water and landed at the front of the roof, reaching out to grab one of the drone's arms.

The drone had no face to express emotions, but David had the impression of an annoyed creature swatting a fly as it swept one of its arms and whacked him in the shoulder, sending him tumbling back. He flipped end over end and skidded along the ocean floor.

"Be careful," Sharmila said. "That thing could crack your faceplate."

David nodded. She was right. Down here the pressure was *immense*—if his pressurized suit were punctured, it would crumple and implode, turning him into nothing more than a trace of himself inside whatever tiny wreck of his suit was left.

"Shoot it!" David cried, raising his weapon at the same time Sharmila did. They both fired, and this time their bolts were true, striking the drone smack in the center. The drone began to bounce, one of its legs going haywire and flying back.

David fired again, and this time the drone split apart. A burst of flame issued from the silver ball and hissed in the water.

"Got it," Sharmila said, but *no*, David didn't think they had gotten it at all.

The top of the silver globe was spinning, not with the momentum of the bolt but entirely on its own. An egglike portion, the top of the globe, spun itself free and lifted off. As it rose high, quickly escaping, the rising top dragged a tail, a long silvery cable that David now realized had reached through the drill leg and into the body of the rover. As the egg lifted into the sea and rose, the cable trailed after it, shortening, reeling itself in.

Sharmila and David stared up into the darkness, watching the rising drone disappear.

And then the rover rumbled. The husk of the drone scattered and fell down the hood, landing at David's feet.

He glanced at it and back up at the rover and heard a distinct *pop* as the drilled hole in the roof burst inward. "Get down," David called.

He and Sharmila dropped to the silty ocean floor as the rover began to shake, and then the skin of the vehicle, powerful enough to withstand a rocket-propelled grenade, split open and ripped itself inward as the ocean proved its superiority to the works of man.

The rover groaned, its wheels lifting off the silt, and then all at once it crunched itself into a ball of metal the size of a refrigerator.

Sharmila started and then looked up, as though they could still see the drone.

"Good Lord," she said. "What *was* that?" But she wasn't talking about the implosion, David realized. That was bound to happen the moment something drilled through the roof.

"I have no idea." He shook his head.

He turned away from the imploded vehicle to watch the Lodgers, who were done with their feeding and heading off to amuse themselves however they saw fit. Sharmila servoed her way next to him and tilted her helmet back at the wrecked rover. "What do you think *that* was about?"

David looked back. He was thinking of the snaking cable that drew itself into the fleeing drone. And the computers inside the rover, with their open connecting ports. "I'm not sure. But I'm worried that it got whatever it wanted."

1

"I'VE GOT IT ... Gabe, I've got it." Peter Kosydar's voice cracked excitedly as he picked up the remnants of the cardboard insert of a T-shirt. He uncapped a marker and started to scrawl, bumping into the table with the model on it along the way.

Gabriel Nemo grabbed on to the edge of the glass-topped desk Peter had bumped into and steadied the table. A two-inch G.I. Joe figure of a US Marine toppled over, and Gabriel righted it again. The Marine figure sat in a little cardboard captain's chair in the center of a model they'd been cobbling together from whatever they could get their hands on in their room for hours. Ever since Peter had woken Gabriel up in the middle of the night with inspiration—a lot of inspirations, in fact. They'd set to work immediately.

Little bits of plastic and cardboard littered the desk around the model. In cardboard miniature lay the bridge of the submarine *Obscure*. Its floor was an oval cut from the T-shirt cardboard. The faceplate of their only room clock, detached and held up by toothpicks, indicated the view screen at the front.

Peter tapped the cardboard he was drawing on and picked up a pair of scissors. Over his shoulder, warm sunlight speckled the surface of the water outside the Nemo Institute, just over the horizon from California. The sight of the choppy blue and a distant dolphin leaping and diving warmed Gabriel's heart, and he looked back at Peter, who was cutting out long rectangles along which he had scrawled the numbers *3.5'* on the side and *5'* across the top.

"What are those?"

"Walls."

"In the middle of the bridge?"

Peter pushed back his glasses. His blond hair was matted and irregular, as though he were wearing a crown of straw. He placed the pieces of cardboard behind the sections of the bridge. "We've got the room. We already decided we'll take a lot of equipment and put it in the new egress hatch next to your captain's chair."

"Yeah, but we might need more room for that," Gabriel said. "How am I gonna spin around?" Gabriel turned the

Marine sitting in the captain's chair and had to stop. "See? My legs hit this new wall over the egress hatch."

"So maybe it's just the hatch there," Peter answered. "Plus, seriously, the cardboard is not to scale; that action figure's legs look about seven feet long."

That seemed right. Gabriel moved the action figure over by the view screen and saw that, indeed, the sizes were all wrong. "Okay, so tell me about the walls."

"We have a five-foot-long wall behind Misty's station and another behind mine." Peter pointed. "The walls are three and a half feet tall, two feet thick. I say we make them hollow. So we can open them up and use them."

"As... shelves?"

"Yeah. Yeah!" Gabriel looked down. He kicked a stray shoe aside as he circled the table. The shoe landed somewhere with a soft wallop. The room was a disaster, uniform pants and shirts strewn over every possible ledge, unrecognizable crumbs dotting every surface. Peter had covered the walls with movie posters that stretched back a hundred years, such that their friend Misty had said it looked like a movie theater snack bar that hadn't been cleaned in years. That didn't mean anything to Gabriel. But he loved it. "We could store emergency supplies right there. That way in a pinch we wouldn't need to run back to the dive room."

"And a bigger refrigerator could go in the little wall the Marine hit his legs on," Peter added.

Gabriel nodded. That was a great idea. The cooler he had to the right of his chair now was a poor excuse for storage if they were gone for days—even though a long trip like that was rare.

So far they'd covered changes to the view screen, communications equipment, and flooring, and now they were all the way into storage.

"It's amazing," Gabriel said. "I thought the design was perfect when we rolled out the *Obscure*." That was a year ago.

"Well, you didn't have a crew to give you more ideas."

Gabriel folded his arms over his navy-blue T-shirt. "I guess that's true."

"And," Peter said, "we can *decorate* the shelves." He looked up. "You know?"

"Decorate it? Like with *The Blob* posters?"

"What, there's a Nemo regulation against Technicolor? Sure! Misty's, too." Peter moved over next to Gabriel and indicated her station. "Oh," he said abruptly as though just getting an idea. He turned around and ran to the corner of the room, rummaging through a stack of school papers. He came back with two tiny pieces of colored paper, which he rolled into balls, one pink and one green. He put the pink ball on the cardboard that indicated Misty's station on the *Obscure*—ops and weapons— and the green on the floor behind her spot. He picked up a Sharpie and quickly drew a long rectangle. "Imagine there's a wall there."

"What's the pink...?"

"It's the Troll doll," Peter said. Misty had stuck a wild-haired doll to her station a few weeks ago.

Gabriel snorted because he loved that the Troll was now built into their model. "What's the green ball?"

"It's a plant," Peter said. "Haven't you seen her room? She has plants."

"Sure, okay." Gabriel ran his fingers through his hair. "But how are you gonna secure a plant when we go into a steep dive?"

Peter smirked. "I don't know, Gabe, but you've got antique globes in your study, so I'm sure we can learn from that." Since they had started traveling together months ago—even before they had created the Nemo Institute—Peter had been a natural at navigating the *Obscure*. Which was pretty remarkable when you considered that on land, Peter was afraid of water. Like deathly afraid, so afraid he couldn't even drink it. But he was at home on the bridge.

Gabriel stepped back, looking at the model. "So, walls. Is it..."

"What?" Peter was hunched over and stood up.

"I mean, is it bridgelike?"

"Bridgelike?" Peter asked. "It's *your bridge. Our bridge,* if you don't mind. We kinda get to say what's bridgelike. Oh, and did I mention you've already got your own *study?* It looks like a Sherlock Holmes movie in there, how bridge-like is that?"

"Guys!" Misty Jensen pushed the door open, looking in. "Hey!"

"*Door!*" Gabriel and Peter said at the same time. Peter waved his hands wildly. "We could be changing in here."

Misty leaned in the doorway and rolled her eyes. She was wearing her school uniform, a green tunic over black pants. She looked impatient. "Do you realize you missed—what's that?" She ran over to the model. "This is the bridge?"

Peter nodded. "With some improvements."

"Ooh, I have a plant," she cooed at the little green ball. She looked at the whiteboard. "And I get a *wall.* You get a wall! You want to put posters on your wall. Oh, guys, I like this with the walls." She grinned, her massive mane of curly hair bouncing.

Peter pointed. "You've still got your changing room, but we've moved it behind your station instead of mine. We made the space by moving equipment into this station the Marine figure keeps bumping into."

Misty picked up the pink Troll doll–representing ball. "How long have you guys been at this?"

Gabriel shrugged. He looked back at the sunlight on the water outside. His wristband was in the pocket of the pants he had left draped over the leg of the bunk bed and he hadn't bothered to retrieve it. "Since … what, four?"

"Four," Peter said.

"So, like, I guess, three hours? It feels like nothing."

Misty nodded. "Okay, but it wouldn't be three hours; it's *four* hours," Misty said. "You missed yoga *and* breakfast." Misty was a devoted student of exercise and health, especially now that she'd been taking an exercise science course at the Nemo Institute that would have been advanced for a high school senior, much less a middle schooler. Though it had made her prone to toss out nuggets of exercise wisdom like she was everybody's personal trainer.

"What?" Peter asked.

"It's *eight o'clock*," Misty yelped, suddenly standing up and looking at her Nemotech wristband. "That was what I was gonna tell you."

Argh. Gabriel turned and yanked his own wristband out of the pants. "We took the alarm apart…"

Peter fished his own band out of a jumble of tech on the other desk. "Oh, you're right." He looked at Misty. "Some help you are."

Gabriel pulled on his tunic over his T-shirt and flicked his hands at Misty. "Out, out, we gotta move."

"Wait for us," Peter called.

"Ninety seconds," Misty answered. "We have six minutes to get to class. I'm not gonna be late because—"

Gabriel grabbed his pants and shooed her into the hall. He pulled on the pants, asking Peter, "Are you changing?"

Peter was wearing a pair of ratty blue basketball shorts

and a T-shirt that read ALTS IZ FARLOYRN. *All is lost*, apparently. The first line ever spoken by an actor Peter liked. He looked down and shrugged. "I'm good." He sat and yanked on some shoes, sockless. "We can finish this later."

Misty was waiting in the hall, and they started running together. "How could you not know the time?"

"We got distracted," Gabriel said.

"School starts the same time every day," she said, sounding more like her air force parents than herself. "Don't forget we're down in the viewing hall on Fridays."

Gabriel winced. His mom's marine biology class was the first class they had, and Fridays were special because class was held in a Nemoglass-encased hall below the surface. She'd be *so* upset if he were late. Argh. It would put her in a spot where it would look like she was playing favorites if she didn't call him out on it. Guilt washed through him. He was usually the first person there.

His mom would be furious.

No—disappointed. And that was *worse*.

They ran down the Nemo Institute's main tower.

It wasn't just any tower, either. Rising two hundred feet above the surface of the Pacific, the Manta II tower swirled with blue glass from its base up to a seventy-foot-wide, three-story house of crystal and blue in the shape of a manta ray. It was very similar to the tower it was named after, the one at Nemolab. The crystal was Nemoglass, the unique, incredibly strong transparent material the family used for the windows of Nemotech ships and the massive domes of the lab. At the surface and below, the tower was surrounded by a tight cluster of twenty-foot-wide tubes gathered close together, resembling a great coral pipe cluster stretching to the sky. It also, to Gabriel's eye, looked like a pipe organ, the kind that once rested (or so he was told) in the stateroom of the original Captain Nemo aboard the original Nemoship, *Nautilus*. Fittingly the building was called the Pipes.

They reached the end of the hall and entered a large stairwell that ran along a great glass wall, and Gabriel brought them all to a halt. He craned his neck to look out. Peter and Misty pressed their foreheads to the glass. In the distance he could see the shadow of a metal latticework covered in seaweed, intended to one day become a new coral reef. Already it was a feeding ground for countless kinds of fish and crabs.

Just barely, Gabriel could see down to the corner of a great white building at the bottom of the tower. An enormous glass dome showed itself at the corner, the rest of it underwater. He could make out the shapes of the students already gathered, below the waterline in the dome. Against the wall, his mother consulted her notes on a tablet. Class was about to start.

He tapped the glass as they kept moving. "Time?"

"Got about three minutes," Misty said.

Gabriel hopped on a long silver handrail and slid down to the next landing. Outside, the surface of the water cut across the glass.

When they hit the next level, Peter held up a hand. "Wait, left, left." And he and Gabriel were gone through a pair of double swinging doors. The cafeteria.

"There's no *time*," Misty growled. But she ran after them.

"It's a shortcut," Gabriel shouted back.

"It's true," Peter said as he shot through the double doors. "Through the kitchen there's a hallway that leads to the lecture hall. Plus I'm *famished*."

The cafeteria was quiet as a tomb, the lights flickering on to reveal a wide room of long silver tables. The floor-to-ceiling windows revealed pylons of concrete where schools of fish shot by in streams of color. Gabriel and Peter raced to the back, near the kitchen, where a tray of forlorn breakfast rolls had still not been taken in. Peter grabbed three and tossed one over his shoulder to Gabriel.

Misty pointed out the window on the right—beyond the thick glass and the water they could see the classroom dome.

They burst into the kitchen, and Gabriel waved at Mr. Francesco, the head cook, who was going over something on a clipboard with two of his staff. All of them wore white. Mr. Francesco looked at the three students in surprise and barely had a moment to speak before they were gone again, out the door in the back of the kitchen.

As they poured into the hallway, Peter pitched Gabriel a little bottle of orange juice.

"Where'd you get this?"

"It was on the table next to Mr. Francesco."

Down corridors of black marble, they slid to the next stairwell and down silvery guardrails. Finally, they reached the bottom and a pair of double doors that read SEA OBSERVATION.

Gabriel, Peter, and Misty breathed for a second, and then Misty pushed on in.

They entered a dome thirty feet wide and mostly underwater, with black tiles on the floor and a world of sea life teeming all around. The three careened to a halt at the back of the students, who were all standing, waiting for Mom to look up. The doors clicked shut behind them.

"And that's time," Misty said.

"Shortcuts." Gabriel and Peter shared a fist bump as Gabriel's mom looked up and rose, smiling at the class.

"Good morning," she said, her voice a gorgeous lilt of Hindi- and French-tinged English. She swept her bright eyes over the crowd, briefly connecting with Gabriel's. "The reason we're meeting in this hall today is because I wanted us to have a view of the sea life just outside. Today we're going to talk about changing mammal behavior due to global shifts in temperature."

Gabriel nodded. His mother had been talking to him for as long as he could remember about how tiny rises in average temperature could damage sea life. It was one of her regular topics (he would almost call them *sermons*) when he and his sister were younger.

On cue, a great white shark, taller than Gabriel, whisked by the window, whipping its tail and curling away. "Oh, well, there," Mom said. For a moment her eyes took on a sad, faraway look that automatically made Gabriel's eyes water. He could handle the idea that Earth was in danger, but he couldn't stand her to be sad. "That shark's not really strange to see. But at this time of year, with the water cooling in the fall, I'd expect most of these sharks to have moved south to Baja. The waters off Southern California are a sort of nursery for sharks, and we've seen increasing shark presence in the shallow waters as the water has stayed warmer, longer." She turned back. "Now, sharks don't really like attacking people, but if it happens at all, it will happen more as the water warms."

"Well *that's* a great message to kick off the day with," Peter whispered.

"Shh," Misty said.

"But sharks are survivors," Mom said. "The coral reefs,

on the other hand—" Mom looked up as she was cut off by a blaring alarm Klaxon that Gabriel felt in his bones.

What the heck was that? Gabriel barely recalled that there even were Klaxons at the school, though of course there were. But he couldn't imagine why someone would trigger it unless something huge had happened, like a pleasure boat crashing into the side of the school.

"What on Earth?" Mom yelled over the alarm sound. She went to the lectern and touched a button. "This is Dr. Nemo! What's happening?"

A voice came on that Gabriel recognized as one of the security personnel in the control room of the Manta II tower. "Perimeter alarm!" he shouted. "Dr. Nemo, there's something big coming toward us. Or at least it *was* coming toward us. Now it's stopped. We're picking up a faint SOS. Did you copy that?"

"It's sending an emergency signal?" Mom asked. *SOS* was universal code for *help us*. No one really knew what *SOS* stood for. There was a lot of talk that it stood for *Save Our Ship*, but like a lot of things about the sea, that probably wasn't true. "What is it?"

"It's a submarine," the voice replied. "And they've stopped six miles off."

"A submarine? And you said it was a big one?" The word could mean anything, but for submarines, *big* would mean enormous, several hundred feet in length. Gabriel instantly thought of his sister—she had a big submarine. Mom had the same thought, apparently: "Is it the *Nebula?*"

"No." The voice sounded confused. "It's not one of ours." Not a Nemo submarine, he meant. Not sending out any of the familiar Nemo codes or showing a Nemotech profile, visually or even in how the hull reflected the pings of sonar. Anyway, as far as Gabriel knew, there were currently only two Nemo submarines, and one of them was docked below the Institute.

Gabriel turned to Peter and Misty. "SOS," he whispered.

"Everyone, take a moment." Mom held up her hands as if she could calm the class with her palms.

"Dr. Nemo, if you could have a look at this," the voice said.

Mom shook her head slightly. "Of course. Class? I expect you to read the articles I've posted on your class pages, and if you were wise, you'd take the rest of the period to do that. I'm sorry to leave you. We'll continue Monday!"

Mom tucked her tablet under her arm and hurried through the room, her dark blue flats clicking on the black tile. She passed Gabriel and squeezed his shoulder as she went. Then the class was alone.

"So, are we going to read?" someone asked, but even a bunch of STEM geeks were still human. They stampeded out of the room like cattle, intent on being anywhere but a classroom if they had the chance.

24

"What do you think?" Peter whispered as they moved with the crowd. He, Gabriel, and Misty kept their heads close together.

"An SOS?" Misty answered. "*I* want to have a look."

"Absolutely," Gabriel said. "Let's just make sure we can lose the crowd."

It was time to go *Obscure*.

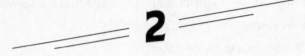

2

THEY NEEDED TO get to the *Obscure*, but they were on the wrong side of the building. The Nemo Institute had a hangar at the water level for docking boats and even the small submarines that the Institute sometimes used for moving about, including the one Gabriel's mom used when she needed to travel back to Nemobase. Every one of the eighty students and myriad staff knew and used that dock.

The *Obscure* dock was hidden and unknown to all but a few people. Gabriel and his crew needed to get there without being noticed.

They were still surrounded by students as Gabriel flipped a panel on the side of his wristband, pulled out a small earpiece, and slipped it into his ear. "Mr. Dorn?" He tried not to raise his voice, but the still-ringing alarms made it hard for him to hear.

"Gabriel?" A deep voice, the same one that had called out to Mom from the control room, responded. Mr. Dorn—a muscular, ex–Navy SEAL giant—was the most physically imposing man Gabriel had ever seen, and even his voice was a little scary.

"You're about to have a minor glitch with the security systems where it will look like a hangar door opened, but, uh, it didn't, and you didn't hear it from me."

"Hear what from you?"

"Perfect," Gabriel said. He gave the thumbs-up to Misty and Peter. They kept time with the other students, who were moving in pairs and threes through a door at the end of the corridor. "Library," he said.

They went through the doors and climbed a flight of stairs, still surrounded by students. They stopped at the first landing, letting a bunch of their classmates pass them. They needed a lull before any more students came. Gabriel didn't want anyone seeing which way he and his crew went. When they had the stairs to themselves, they dashed through a door marked LEVEL I. All the students' rooms were higher up, but no one paid attention to the three of them disappearing here.

They came out in another corridor with glass on one side, looking out from about twelve feet above the water. Misty ran ahead, hitting the double glass doors to a room with huge stacks of books inside. The word *library* was etched into the glass of the door.

The library of the Nemo Institute was practically empty at this time of day, save for the Library Sisters, a pair of seventy-something women in matching berets who, as far as Gabriel knew, had been installed with the library itself. Apparently, they were old friends of the family. They barely looked up at Misty, Gabriel, and Peter as the students ran past the counter. The three zipped around couches and tables and countless little green lamps before making their way to a shelf in the back labeled OCEANIC HISTORY.

They gathered behind the history shelf, dwarfed by eleven feet of ancient books. On the other side were shorter shelves and a glass wall. Misty touched the glass and whispered, as she always did, "Hi, Mom," because from here you could see all the way to California.

"Can I do it?" Peter asked. "I never get to do it."

"Be my guest," Gabriel said.

They stopped for a moment, a narrow shelf in front of them, the glass wall on one side and the tall shelf on the other. In front of the shelf, on a three-foot pedestal, sat a model of Granite House, a cliffside home once inhabited by friends of the Nemos on a faraway South Pacific island. Tiny windows were cut into the stone, and at the mouth of a cave near the top of the cliff was a tiny model campfire.

Waves crashed against the foot of the cliff, and a beach grew along the sides, with a tiny drawbridge over a little river that flowed off and disappeared from the sculpture.

Peter reached out, touched a hidden button under the pedestal, and then put two fingers under the drawbridge, flipping it up. He stepped back, as did Gabriel and Misty.

With a mechanical whine, the section of the floor below the pedestal dropped away, the pedestal becoming the topmost part of the center column of a spiral staircase.

Lights sprang on as they descended into the staircase, stepping hurriedly past concrete pillars and countless pipes sending water and power to the school. They emerged onto a landing at the bottom and stood before a door bearing a large circular wheel. Misty touched her palm to a glass reader at the center of the wheel, and after a few chirps, it began to spin.

The metal door suddenly flew up, disappearing into the ceiling. Gabriel felt his heart leap, even though he knew what he would see. There, beyond a concrete walkway, floated the *Obscure*.

The Nemoship glistened in the dim light with black plates inlaid with stripes of mother-of-pearl. At first all Gabriel could see in the dark hangar were faint reflections from the stripes on the hull. Gabriel hopped onto the platform on the nose of the submarine. He used his hand-print to open the hatch. Gabriel climbed down, his friends following quickly after, lights flickering on as they hopped to the floor. Less than five minutes after hearing the alarms, they were inside the bridge.

The bridge of the *Obscure* was the nerve center of the ship. It was where the commander of the ship had at his beck and call all the major systems and the officers in charge of them—navigation, weapons, life support. On US Navy submarines, such places were called control rooms, but on very old ships they were called the *bridge*, and the name had stuck for the Nemos. The *Obscure* bridge was oval-shaped and toward the front of the ship. It had no windows or portholes—instead the crew relied on a large view screen that, besides its ability to show sonar and maps and pretty much anything the crew could pull up from the internet, displayed whatever was shown by a collection of cameras mounted around the ship.

But it was more than that. The bridge of the *Obscure* was Gabriel's home, more than anywhere else. More so even than the multiple-domed underwater complex at the bottom of the sea where he'd spent most of his life. It was the place where he felt truly alive.

As he arrived, Gabriel began flipping on the engines and interior lights. He pulled a tablet from its cradle on the front wall, right under the view screen, and opened a checklist that they had to go through every time they took the ship out. Misty and Peter chattered as they went to their stations.

"You got Navs on?" Peter called as he slid into the helm seat and snapped his restraints over his shoulders and waist. *Navs* was short for navigation, the systems the crew used to determine and control the direction and speed of the ship.

"Yeah." Gabriel paced as they ran through their checklists.

Misty dropped into her spot—operations, defense, basically everything that wasn't navigation. "Lemme take over the checklist?"

"You bet." Gabriel leaned on the back of his own seat. Each of them needed practice doing the others' jobs. Peter's was navigation, but he needed to be able to run Misty's defenses even if he wouldn't normally be called to. Gabriel, in command, needed to be able to do everything.

Misty called out, "Prepare to dive."

"Prepare to dive, aye," Peter echoed. Engines in the walls of the *Obscure* chugged to life, filling the tanks in the walls with heavy liquid. They would need to dive down and exit through a hangar door about twice as wide and half again as high as the *Obscure*. Gabriel felt the ship drop and spin around as Peter pointed the nose down toward the exit.

"Dive," Misty said, and Peter echoed her as they dropped like a stone, the engines taking the ship as they zipped down and out into the sea.

Half the view screen showed the front cameras, dim green water that swam with colorful sea life. They began to move at flank speed, regular speed for piloting near anything that would be dangerous to hit, like another craft or a school of fish.

"Wring her out," Misty said. "Full speed."

Front lamps lit up the water as they began to move toward the image on the sonar screen. The *Obscure* began to move, and as Gabriel watched the water move faster past the view screen, he felt more at home than he ever had in his life. "Sonar," he said. "Let's see who our visitors are."

"Sonar online," Peter said. "There you go." The giant view screen sparkled to life as pings of sound went shooting through the water and bounced back to the ship, mapping out the area and showing up on a circular map.

"There it is," Peter said. On the screen was a large shadow, slowly moving in their direction, now about four miles away.

"How big is that?" Gabriel asked.

"Three hundred feet, I'd estimate. And loud." Peter flipped a switch, and now the sound he was hearing on his own earpiece came through over the speakers on the bridge of the *Obscure*. The distant engines churned, clanging and scraping loudly.

"That is the strangest thing I've ever heard." Gabriel scrunched his face.

"I doubt that's true," Misty observed.

"It is weird, though," Peter agreed. "That clanging sounds

like something in their rotors is damaged. That's one reason we can see them so well on the sonar—we're getting way more sound than you'd usually have from even a big sub like that."

"Is it navy?"

"Nope, at least not US Navy." Misty flipped through reports on the navy subs in the Pacific. "Not likely, anyway. All the subs this close to the coast are accounted for."

"Well, they don't make everything public," Gabriel observed. Locations of US Navy subs were generally secret, although the navy made it known roughly where the ships were.

"You ever hear a navy engine sound like that?"

"You can turn that off." Gabriel winced at the agonizing sound of the strange rotors. "They sent an SOS; that's all we need."

"They were approaching the Institute before they stopped." Peter cut the sound of the strange sub.

"Institute, this is *Obscure*," Gabriel called. "Peter, how soon will we reach it?"

"About six minutes," Peter said.

"Institute." Mom's voice came back.

"We're underway to meet the vessel; have you guys gotten a message beyond the SOS?"

"Nothing," Mom said.

"Here neither, but it's strange, it sounds like they have

engine trouble." Gabriel looked back at Misty. "Maybe we can try and talk to them. Mom, we'll contact you when we know more."

Misty moved a slider on her screen, choosing a different channel, and spoke slowly and clearly. "Unknown vessel, this is Nemoship *Obscure*. Come in?" She shrugged at Gabriel.

Peter scoffed. "Gabe, this is weird."

"They could be hurt," Gabriel said. He sighed. If the vessel had suffered a hull breach, the strangers could be in big trouble. "Institute, we should arrive in five."

"Mr. Nemo," came the voice of Mr. Dorn. "You should be careful."

Gabriel shrugged his shoulders elaborately as he turned to Misty and Peter. "Are we not always careful?" He called back, "Copy."

"I'm just saying, they may be in trouble, but it's still a submarine."

Gabriel understood. Submarines often had weapons, and the last thing they needed was someone torpedoing the *Obscure* because they were taken by surprise or malfunctioning. He got up and went to Misty's station, touching the call button. "Unknown vessel, do you need assistance?"

"They're diving," Peter said. "A little. And moving laterally."

"To do what?" Misty asked. "To get away from us?"

"I don't know," Peter said.

"Put us on a path fifty feet above them. How long till we meet them?"

"Four minutes."

"Unknown vessel, I say again—"

Now there was a cry of voices, several at once, impossible to make out. The sound burst over the speakers. Several people shouted indiscernible messages amid loud, rushing sounds behind them. Then it cut out.

"I think they're in trouble," Gabriel said. "Unknown vessel, we are coming to meet you. Peter, adjust so that we can come right alongside them when we meet them."

"We can see them now." Peter threw the image onscreen. Across the water a mile and a half away, a long, flattish submarine moved through the water, tilted, one side of its tapered face about twenty degrees above the other.

"Do you see markings?" Gabriel asked.

"I don't," Peter said.

Misty said, "That's not *any* navy ship. It's some kind of private sub. Like us. What do you want to do?"

Gabriel shook his head. "What are the options for rescuing people off a sub?"

Misty looked grave. "Not very good. Best is if you can get them to surface and fix their engines."

"You can't haul them," Peter said. "Don't even think it."

"Could we set up an umbilical between the ships for people to climb through?"

"They could have hundreds of crew," Peter said. "But yes. Okay . . . we're on them."

"Unknown vessel," Gabriel said, "do you read? We are nearby and prepared to render assistance . . ." He turned to Peter. "Put the engine sounds back on?"

The sound of the clanging engines came back as the *Obscure* slowed, moving steadily with the strange submarine fifty feet below them in the water. It was painted dull gray, with no markings he could see and a very thin tail halfway across the back.

As they reached the back of the three-hundred-foot vessel, the sound of the engines grew more erratic.

"She's *rupturing*," Peter said with alarm, and indeed, the tail of the gray sub began to bend outward as if being pushed from inside.

"Prepare to deploy flotation devices," Gabriel said. If crewmen went into the water, there was some chance that the *Obscure* might be able to save them. "Get us close."

"How close?" Peter asked.

"Close as you can."

Misty gasped. "Maybe we can get under them, like nudge them toward the surface."

"It's an idea. That would make it safer for everyone aboard. Peter, is it possible?"

He nodded. "Yes, but we gotta be real easy about it."

"Go."

Peter dipped the *Obscure* toward the sub, moving downward. It was an absurd idea, but if there were people to save, it was what they would do.

"Okay, we're gonna impact," Peter said. "As slow as we can. Brace...ten seconds."

They came closer. But then the new submarine began to spin away, jostling. And then—

"What's it *doing*?" Misty cried. "Oh, those poor people."

It shook apart. Gabriel gasped out loud. At first, as the seams of the tail split open and the panels along the top separated, Gabriel held his breath for fear that a great ball of expanding gas from an engine explosion was about to send the *Obscure* end over end. But no: The strange vessel's engine, a propeller inside a cage, shook loose, rattling like a windup toy. It spun into the depths as the panels of the ship sloughed off and began to float. Soon the *Obscure* was surrounded by a rising tide of floating panels that had been the submarine.

"Wait, wait, wait," Gabriel said, his fear for the crew members melting into complete confusion.

The vessel had simply come apart as though made of cardboard.

"What the heck?" Gabriel asked.

Peter zoomed in toward one of the panels as it tumbled past the front camera. It seemed to be made of cheap material, foam and plastic.

The sound of the engine disappeared as it stopped, presumably at the bottom of the sea.

37

"It was a *fake*," Misty said. "But *why*? What would be the *point*?"

Gabriel watched the panels float toward the surface.

What *would* be the point?

The point would be to call for a rescue.

To bring the rescuers out here.

The point would be to draw the *Obscure* away.

"Call the Institute," Gabriel demanded.

Misty nodded. "Nemo Institute, this is *Obscure*. We have something really strange."

They waited for a few moments. Nothing.

Misty repeated her call.

Gabriel folded his arms. "Oh, I don't like this."

"We're getting a *text* message," Misty said.

Words began tapping across the bottom of the screen, meaning someone who couldn't access the microphone at the control panel still had access to a Nemo Communicator.

OBSCURE THIS IS INSTITUTE

SOS

WE ARE UNDER ATTACK

3

"**WHO'S SENDING THAT** SOS?" Misty asked. She tapped words that jostled onto the screen. "Who is this?"

No answer.

"We were suckers," said Gabriel. He was ashamed that he'd been fooled, and it made him want to howl.

"Nope," Peter said. "Someone tricked us. There's a difference."

"Just—"

"If you're gonna say *get us back to the school*, I'm already on it," Peter said. "Buckle up or hang on."

Gabriel heard the engines rumble as the *Obscure* picked up speed. Heavy liquid sloshed out of the tanks, lifting the craft as it went, allowing Peter to use the craft's desire to shoot to the surface to get even more speed out of her. But they were still ten minutes away at least.

Peter looked at the screen and called, "Brace yourselves—we got a boat in our way." He yanked the stick, and the *Obscure*'s bridge tilted sideways as he steered clear of a large pleasure craft in their path, its lower points as deep as the *Obscure* itself. The blue steel of the boat sailed past the cameras as they swept around it, then they shot forward again. On the sonar screen, they were a fast-moving dot headed for the Nemo Institute, which flashed dully, revealing nothing of whatever trouble they were in.

Once he seemed satisfied with their path, Peter looked up from Gabriel to Misty. He took off his glasses and pointed with them at the screen, as though it were the source of their first message.

"Anyway," Peter said, "we weren't suckers. We were tricked. Suckers deserve what they get. We were tricked, because whoever it was knew we were going to go to someone's rescue. We go where the trouble is. Okay? What would you want, that we don't go?" He waited for a moment.

Gabriel looked down. He wasn't used to Peter being so wise. "I'm just saying..."

"We don't *not go*," Peter said. "We went, we saw what we did, we turned around, and now we're moving as fast as we can."

"Okay," Gabriel said. "Good grief. Who taught you to make speeches like that?"

"It's from listening to *you* for months on end," Misty muttered. She studied the text again. "So *now* what do we know? 'SOS, we are under attack.' From what?"

"Could be from anything," Gabriel said. "Could be another submarine."

"We didn't see another sub on the scope," Peter said. "But yeah."

"Could be helicopters, could be regular ships. But whoever they were, they were smart enough to lure us out here with a fake sub."

Misty said, "Yeah, someone knows how we work." That someone knew about the Institute and knew they had a submarine to defend them.

A beeping sound erupted from Peter's helming station.

Peter tapped the screen. "There's another ship."

"Onscreen."

The main screen filled with the sonar image of their quadrant of the Pacific. A green dot was moving steadily in their direction, fleeing the Institute.

Peter picked up a big, padded pair of earphones and listened. "No. That's a sub."

"Another one?" Gabriel asked. "Okay, so is *this* one navy?"

Misty looked up from her screen. "No. I'm running the sound of its engines through our recognition routines. It's another weird stranger."

Something about that made Gabriel pause. He felt like

the world was becoming unfamiliar fast. "Uh...can you tell how big it is?"

Peter watched the sonar line sweep around the circle onscreen and around again. "Judging by how long it takes to form that dot, I'd say you're looking at a typhoon-sized ship."

"What?"

Typhoon-sized. *Typhoon*, as in the name of a group of submarines that tended to be enormous—about 575 feet long. Not to be trifled with. And if this ship was that big but they couldn't recognize it, that was really unnerving, because they had no idea who might be inside it.

Gabriel looked at Peter. "If it's not navy, and it's not a Nemoship..."

The radio crackled and Mr. Dorn's voice came on. "*Obscure!* Institute to *Obscure.* Come in!"

"We're here," Misty said into her screen.

"What happened?" Gabriel asked anxiously.

"The Institute was hit by a vessel that came up from below, minutes after you left, but—do you see it? Do you have that sub?" There was an urgency and worry in Mr. Dorn's voice that was completely unfamiliar to Gabriel. He had never heard Mr. Dorn speak with anything other than something close to boredom, even in emergencies.

"We've got something on sonar," Gabriel said. "A big stranger."

"Stop it. You have to stop it. But listen." Mr. Dorn's voice was insistent. "Cripple it. Don't destroy it. Do you understand? *Don't destroy it.*"

Gabriel didn't have any plans to destroy anything or anyone. But he didn't like the sound in Mr. Dorn's voice. "Why, what's the problem?"

"Just . . . *stop it* before it gets out to sea, Mr. Nemo," Mr. Dorn said. "I'll tell you more when you're back."

"If—" Gabriel started and stopped, thinking. When he spoke again, he had lowered his voice. A submarine revealed itself mainly by sound. Even voices inside a sub could be heard through the water. If the *Obscure* were to have any chance, everyone needed to stop shouting at one another. "If you want me to catch a sub, Mr. Dorn, we need to stop talking. Switch to text." Gabriel nodded, and Misty turned off the radio, WE ARE UNDER ATTACK still displayed on the bottom of the screen.

Gabriel looked back at Peter and whispered, "Intercept course."

"Laying in an intercept course, aye," Peter whispered back, pushing buttons.

The green dot was moving fast as it fled the Institute, and now the dot indicating the *Obscure* altered course slightly to move toward it.

"Their time to our position?" Gabriel watched the screen, meaning *How far away are they?*

"At their speed, six minutes," Peter answered.

"Then unless they change course, they're gonna come to us. Kill engines. Go silent." Gabriel stood back. The floor of the bridge leveled off and stopped vibrating as the *Obscure* stopped pulsing forward.

Go silent. Two simple words, a simple order that triggered a cascade of adjustments in the ship as the entire submarine prepared itself to be as invisible as possible. Gabriel said it and Peter triggered it and the world they inhabited became instantly scarier.

The lights on the bridge went dark, replaced by a dim red. Outside, Gabriel knew, the floodlights would be shutting off. The *Obscure* bobbed, drifting in place. They should be nearly invisible now, except that they were still using sonar to grope around them. And that could give them away.

"Kill active sonar," Gabriel whispered. Sonar worked by firing off sound and listening for the sound to bounce back. But now a submarine was coming their way, and that submarine knew that there was another submarine nearby, one they had lured away but might well be on the way back now. So the strangers would be listening for them. Listening for engines, and voices, and sonar. *All* they could do was listen.

Peter took off the headphones and unplugged them, and the sounds of the ocean filled the room.

They heard the swish of the water, slow and steady,

like the current of blood through the body. Peter turned a knob, focusing the microphones, and held up a finger.

They heard pulsing now, the thudding of enormous turbines, muffled but distinct.

There she is, Peter mouthed.

Gabriel listened closer. The engines sounded ... *doubled*.

Peter tapped so that his thoughts were echoed onscreen for both the *Obscure* crew and the Institute. STRANGE ... ENGINE SOUND HAS AN ECHO—TWO SCREWS? *Screws* were the enormous engine propellers at the back of a submarine. So possibly the sub had two engines, which wasn't preposterous.

The engines grew louder, closer.

And then stopped.

Gabriel looked from Misty to Peter, both of whom craned their heads up as if yanked by the sudden quiet. This was far from good. It meant the unknown sub had gone silent as well.

This part of life on a sub hadn't changed since the creation of submerged craft during the American Civil War. You functioned by listening. By feeling with whatever instruments you had. Even now, Gabriel had cameras, and they could add all kinds of new equipment. But eventually cameras didn't see anything useful and you were left exactly where submarine captains had been in World War II or the Civil War or anytime: listening. Reaching out with your imagination, as though you could use your mind as a special kind of sonar and use your guts and your vision to imagine another person, standing on another ship, asking: *What are they thinking, and why? If I were them, what would they be doing next?*

Gabriel realized he was hunching over and stood straight, rolling his shoulders and letting his breath calm.

The *Obscure* and its counterpart were standing still now: two subs feeling in the dark for each other.

They heard a ping, a high-pitched tone, as it bounced and echoed in the water. It rose in pitch and died.

"Can you trace that?" Gabriel whispered.

Peter shook his head, whispering back, "It seemed to come from two places. I don't know how."

Gabriel shook his head in frustration. If the sub out there had sent out a ping and they on the *Obscure* had heard it, then possibly—likely?—the *Obscure* had been made visible by it, outlined by the bouncing of the sound along the hull of the Nemoship. Even now he could envision the captain, getting a signal that the *Obscure* had just come alive on their screen. Or maybe they had failed to get a solid lock on the *Obscure*. In which case the stranger would be scratching his head. Wondering if he should try again.

It didn't matter—Gabriel's job was to stop the strange sub. He must not only avoid attack—he must attack first. He needed to get the sub up on the screen. He turned to Peter when he was certain the sub had missed them. "Prepare to send a ping."

Peter nodded in silence. Gabriel breathed and listened. For a second.

But it was too late.

A howl like a foghorn shot through the water, making the bulkheads hum. It was a sonar sounding, huge, meant to capture lots of detail. They were lit up like a Christmas tree on the strangers' screens now. The sound of the mysterious ship's engines cut on.

They see us.

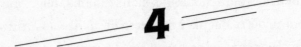

4

"THEY SEE US," Gabriel said urgently and aloud this time. "Battle stations. Start engines. Floodlights. Cameras?"

The bridge lit up as the four views came onscreen. Gabriel spotted the lights of a ship in the starboard view as Peter brought that up to the whole screen.

"Magnify." The camera zoomed.

"*What* the heck is that?" Misty walked forward.

The ship onscreen was unlike any they had ever seen. It was built in two sections—two long bodies, each the size of a large sub and attached to the other by a sleek, shining, ladderlike bridge of metal that ran between the two sub sections. Great engines at the back of each of the sections drove the contraption forward, but

Gabriel could make out multiple little platforms at every corner of the exoskeleton, each sending out a wake that indicated these were adding to the power of the vast machine's engines.

"It's a double sub," Gabriel summed up.

"See any markings?" Misty asked.

"No, so let's call it...uh...the *Twin*. Time for them to reach us?"

"Two minutes."

"Engines slow. Prepare to engage."

"Gabe. They're *really* close."

And before Gabriel could say *I know*, they heard two sounds in rapid succession. The grating noise on the microphones of torpedo bay doors opening on the *Twin* and the sharp whir of a small engine starting up.

On camera, a missile with a long bubbling trail blew out the front of the two sections.

"Torpedo in the water!" Peter shouted.

Gabriel's mind raced. The *Twin* was shooting at them. Now what? "Evasive maneuvers, Peter. Arm pincer torpedoes, Misty."

The *Obscure* lurched upward. For a moment, Gabriel thought the torpedo had no guidance system at all. But no sooner had they moved their bulk up out of its path than it curved its path itself, following them fast.

Gabriel's mind echoed with the odd request from the

Institute: *Don't destroy it.* As if that were even an option: They were about to get blown out of the water. A torpedo—a bomb, basically, a bomb that flew like a dart toward a county fair balloon—was coming straight for them. The result would be the same: A submarine is a hard balloon full of air that moves through the ocean at such depths that any rupture will make it collapse into itself, suddenly and violently.

Gabriel had been in one submarine battle before—one—and it wasn't something he ever wanted to experience again. And he shouldn't—the *Obscure* was an exploration and rescue vessel, not a warship. And yet the strange enemy ship had fired, and the deadly missile was coming their way.

"Time to impact?" Gabriel called.

"Seven seconds."

"Countermeasures." Gabriel looked away from the intercom and spoke to Misty. "Open torpedo bay doors and prepare to fire."

A submarine couldn't hit a torpedo with a torpedo; it wasn't even worth trying. There were only a few things you could do with a torpedo: Let it hit you, get out of the way, or put up something for it to hit instead. The first was almost never a happy ending, but it happened from time to time. The second—getting out of the way—was something they were already doing. Evasive maneuvers.

But a submarine can't turn on a dime, and the torpedo kept coming. The third option, putting up something else for the torpedo to hit, had a name: countermeasures. Targets they would throw out to draw the enemy torpedo away.

"Countermeasures, aye," Misty repeated. "Preparing to fire."

Onscreen, he saw the countermeasures going. From housings on the left and right side of the *Obscure*, small barrels fired off and propelled themselves into the water. Each one had a loud, rattling screw, kicking up clouds of bubbles as they shot out, putting themselves into the path of the oncoming missile.

The torpedo sliced through the top of the cloud of the first countermeasure but caught the second like a scent, turning to charge. It closed on the barrel.

An explosion split open the water and rocked the *Obscure*. The *Twin* was still coming.

Peter spat, "We need to move out of the way, Gabriel. We shouldn't be getting into a battle."

"I know," Gabriel said. "But Dorn said..."

"To stop them? A gigantic submarine? The only way we're stopping them is if our debris chokes them off after they blow us up."

Gabriel's mind raced through the *Obscure*'s options as the ship closed in. They had two torpedo tubes that he could use. He felt sure his weapons—Nemotech pincer-energy torpedoes—wouldn't destroy the ship. But a direct hit could *damage* the sub, even cripple it.

It was time to use them.

"Fine. Fire," Gabriel said.

"Fire," Misty echoed. Gabriel felt a slight tremor as one of the *Obscure*'s torpedoes shot forward into the water from their right side. It closed quickly on the strange doubled vessel.

"Hang on, hang on, the *Twin* is turning," Peter reported.

Gabriel looked up. No. It wasn't just *turning*. It was doing something odd. The pair of subs and the housing around them turned sideways toward the *Obscure*. He studied the ship as Peter magnified the image.

The exoskeleton shell that held the two subs together had its own gun turrets located at the corners of the metal latticework. The turrets turned, and rockets fired—at first Gabriel thought they were firing missiles, but no.

The rockets were there to make the housing move, apparently. The whole yellow-covered latticework lifted off with the thrust of the rockets, pulling away from the twin subs. The torpedo followed it instead of the subs.

Small holes in the corners of the exoskeleton belched clouds of bubbles as inflatable canisters erupted from the holes, tumbling into the water. They were countermeasures.

Amazing. As the exoskeleton maneuvered away from the subs, the canisters drew Gabriel's torpedo toward them.

The *Obscure*'s torpedo burst against the inflatable barrels, sending enormous bubbles into the water around it.

The two actual subs, though, were intact and now sped up, falling in line side by side.

The twin sub configuration was brilliant, Gabriel thought. Each sub could house a crew, but if the crews were rightly sized, they could use the connector complex to evacuate one into the other if needed. Even now the connector powered on like a third ship on its own rotors. It looked like an empty car trailer, tumbling slowly in the water. It was falling behind the subs and trailing slowly after them. He wondered if the shell had its own weapons.

Peter called out, "Gabriel, we *did* have a double sub, and . . . now we still have two subs coming our way."

"Okay, label them *Twin A* and *Twin B*."

"Which one do I target?" Misty asked. "Maybe the pincer torpedoes will scramble their systems."

"*Twin A*," Gabriel decided aloud. "That's the one on our starboard side." The red targeting circle on the screen swiveled and moved over to the smaller sub on the right side.

"Fire torpedo."

"Torpedo away," Misty answered, and a silvery missile

that glowed with shimmering mother-of-pearl spun like a bullet through the water.

Twin A saw it coming and dove, firing countermeasures as it did. The *Obscure*'s missile curved and hit a countermeasure. But it went off close to the sub, and furious arcs of energy swept from the explosion along the hull of the sub. The sub rolled hard to its port.

"They're firing!" Peter called as another torpedo burst from the rolling *Twin A*. But the sub's torpedo got caught up in the pincer arcs and flared, rocking *Twin A* again. The submarine swung wildly in the water.

Pete whistled. "That must have been rough."

Gabriel pictured it. The captain—maybe there was a captain on each of the *Twin* subs—was probably hanging on, trying not to fall over as he or she shouted commands. *Guess what, I'm not supposed to destroy you. It's your lucky day.* As if he would ever just blow a ship out of the water.

Gabriel decided they'd rattled the first *Twin* enough. "Okay, aim for *Twin B*. Ready both tubes," Gabriel said. "Half-capacity." He had to avoid hitting them too hard, even with pincers. A full-capacity torpedo might well break up the ship, and Dorn had said to just stop them, certainly not rupture them.

"Double shot, half-capacity, aye," Misty said. Two more missiles shot out.

Twin B was under a barrage from the *Obscure* now, two

torpedoes coming their way. One of them narrowly missed as it reared up, the torpedo sliding alongside the yellow hull. Gabriel heard the scraping of metal on the *Obscure*'s mics.

Gabriel turned back to *Twin A*. "Fire."

A bleating alarm rose, and Misty shook her head. "Oh, no."

"What is it?"

She looked at him. "Torpedo Tube Two is malfunctioning."

"Another torpedo in the water!" Peter shouted. "*Twin B* fired this time, time to impact twelve seconds." The strangers weren't letting up.

Gabriel ordered them hard to starboard. The whole bridge banked, and he hung on as they leaned at a forty-five-degree angle. "Countermeasures."

"Aye," Misty cried, and the barrels shot out. He saw the missile disappear under the camera on the screen.

He breathed.

"Keep evading the *Twin*," Gabriel said. "Institute, we've shot our last torpedoes. We have to break off." He sighed. "Whatever you're looking for will have to wait."

Mr. Dorn paused for a moment. "Copy. What's your plan?"

"Flank speed, move off." Flank speed was the sub's slowest speed, the basic movement to shift from place to place.

"Torpedo in the water!" Peter shouted. Gabriel felt the ship turning as Peter steered them, but there was a missile curving its way through the water toward them.

"Countermeasures." Gabriel looked up at the intercom.

The torpedo cracked up against their countermeasures, and the blast rolled the *Obscure* again.

"That was the last of our countermeasures." Misty threw her hands up. The torpedo found a countermeasure close to the *Obscure*'s starboard side.

The blast shook Gabriel to his knees, and he scrambled back up to see a sea full of bubbles. Without more countermeasures, they couldn't afford to be around for another volley. "We need to move off. Set a course for the school—"

Peter shouted, "Wait wait wait—the *Twins* are diving!" The bubbles began to clear. The water beyond was empty. Even the exoskeleton shell had taken the opportunity to disappear. Nothing appeared on the scope. The *Obscure* was alone.

The last shot had provided a distraction while the twin subs made their escape. They were probably just deep enough to be below sonar. Gabriel could chase them, of course... but not without defenses.

"Institute," Gabriel said, "we've lost them."

There was a long pause. "Then I'm very sorry," Mr. Dorn came back. "We all are."

Gabriel frowned. "What are you talking about?"

"I'm sorry to have to—"

"Cut it out and tell me," Gabriel growled.

"Your mother. Dr. Nemo was taken captive. She was on that sub."

5

VERTIGO. GABRIEL FELT the blood drain from his face as he took in what Mr. Dorn had said. He felt unsteady on his feet as he cleared his throat. He didn't hear that. It wasn't possible.

"Mr. Dorn, what did you say?" He tried to sound in command, even cool. But it didn't work, and the fear in his own voice frightened him even more.

"Are you ready to receive images?" Mr. Dorn asked. After a pause he followed up. "Gabriel?"

Gabriel shook himself awake. "Yes. Yes, what do you want to show me?"

"All right," Mr. Dorn said.

A beep sounded behind Gabriel, and Misty said, "Putting it up."

On the screen were the same twin subs coming out of the depths toward the school. "This is shortly after you went on your rescue mission," Mr. Dorn said.

"There has to be some mistake," Gabriel said. "How could they get in?"

"They got in right through the wall," Mr. Dorn said. "While Dr. Nemo was in her lab, a small vessel from the sub docked and sawed a hole through the wall, and a team swept her out."

"Swept her out?" Gabriel gasped.

"A small team of commandos came aboard, grabbed her, and exited. The flooding you see was from when these guys left."

Gabriel felt his chest constrict as three men in dark gray suits emerged from a hole blown in the wall of the lab and took Mom by the shoulders. Mom was looking back at the camera as they led her out almost calmly, as if to say, *I know you're seeing this.*

And I expect you to follow.

And then she was gone, and water poured into the lab, lifting papers and overturning beakers.

"Are you sure she didn't go in the water?" Gabriel shouted.

"We're sure," Mr. Dorn said. "They went straight through to a hatch and then pulled away. We had to seal the lab to stop the flooding."

"Whuh..." Gabriel tried to find words. He'd just seen

the sub, he'd just been knocking one of them over with torpedoes. And then he'd let it *get away*. "Why didn't you tell me she was aboard the *Twin* when we were facing it?"

"Because it might have compromised your decision-making, and you were the best chance at stopping the sub."

Gabriel blinked. He didn't have an argument. But he had no idea what to do next. "We're nearly to school," he told Mr. Dorn. "But we need to turn around. We need to go get her. Peter?"

"On it," Peter said. "Let's get out of here."

"Slow to flank speed and prepare to come about."

"Gabriel," Misty said. "We're out of defenses and we have a jammed torpedo bay door. Plus that last blast knocked us pretty hard."

Gabriel slammed his hand down. "No, of course. We have to . . ."

On the screen, the underwater entrance to the Nemo Institute resolved itself from the gray depths.

Someone had his mother.

Someone— *Oh, holy mackerel, what am I thinking?*

"My father!" Gabriel shouted suddenly. "And my sister, do we know if Nerissa and Dad are okay?"

"I've gotten responses," Dorn said. "If you wanna head up to the control room in the tower as soon as you've docked, I think we should all talk."

"You've *heard* from them?" Gabriel wanted to be sure.

"What your sister said wasn't very friendly, but yes," Dorn said. "We have a call in just a few minutes."

Gabriel nodded. He felt so frustrated. If they hadn't been damaged, he could have headed out right now and taken the call from the water. He turned to Misty and Peter. "As soon as we're docked, can you guys restock us and make sure the hull is good to go?"

"Of course," Misty said.

"Good. And then meet me in the tower." He spoke up. "Mr. Dorn? We're nearly there."

The ship dipped as Peter guided it down and up into the entrance to the hangar. As they began to drift toward the surface, Gabriel said in a low voice, "Ask maintenance to swap out the damaged torpedo bay door. Tell them I'm sorry I can't do it." He was agitated, bouncing. He wanted to get up to the office and talk to his dad. Luckily, they had minor repair materials here at the Institute. But if the breach was large, they'd be out of luck. The only place to do heavy work would be at Nemolab or Nemobase, both of which were thousands of miles into the Pacific.

"You bet," Misty said.

"Then come meet me," Gabriel said. He wasn't sure if he'd already said that. Every time he began to think clearly the image of his mother, kidnapped, washed through his head.

"We're docked," Peter said.

Gabriel hurried through the school, but he wasn't seeing anything around him clearly anymore. The speckling brilliant light on the ocean outside the windows of the library shimmered and made him dizzy as he ran.

He reached the control room and burst in.

The first thing he saw was Mr. Dorn, massive and tall, like a tree. Behind him, on the screen, were two faces. On the right, in a box that floated in a field of deep blue, was Nerissa, Gabriel's sister. On the left was their father.

"Gabriel!" Nerissa shouted as soon as she saw him on her screen. "Good." Nerissa was a fugitive, dedicated to living the Nemo life almost exactly as envisioned by their ancestor. On the screen, Gabriel could see half her body as she stood in her private sanctum just off the bridge of her ship, the *Nebula*, which was on the be-on-the-lookout-for lists of every navy on the planet.

"Where are you?" Gabriel asked.

"I'm about six hundred miles out," Nerissa said. "You saw this sub? We need to gather everything we can about it." Even as he nodded, something struck Gabriel as very strange. She was ordering him around like she always did, but there was a softness in his sister's voice that he didn't recognize. A concern that he found deeply frightening.

"I'm so glad you're both safe," Dad said. Dad sounded

strange, too, but it was a strangeness that Gabriel did recognize. Dad was hiding himself now, hiding his feelings in formality, duty, and purpose. Once when Gabriel was very young, a math tutor from India, someone Dad had treated as another son, fell very ill. Dad sat vigil and worked day and night to find the right cure—but the harder he had worked, the less emotion he'd shown. It was as though a blast shield behind Dad's eyes closed to a sliver and stayed that way until the problem passed.

Which was fine for Dad, but he seemed to forget: *The rest of us are outside the shield.*

"I don't understand," Nerissa said. "Who would kidnap Mom?"

"I blame myself," Dad said. Words. No emotion. "I think it might have been the same people who attacked my rover in the Valley of the Lodgers a few days ago."

"Wait, what?" Nerissa asked. "Someone attacked your rover?"

"A drone," Dad said. "Dr. Kassam and I are still analyzing the computer systems to see what might have been taken, if anything."

"We gotta be faster than that," Nerissa said. "From right now, anything happens, anything weird, we gotta tell one another."

"Who was it?" Gabriel asked.

"My best estimate is the Maelstrom," Dad said.

"Signatures in the search protocols their drone used, plus the engineering of the drone, which is clearly based on stolen Nemotech. Yeah. Yeah."

Gabriel and Nerissa looked at each other through the video and then Nerissa asked, "Who's the Maelstrom?"

You don't know, either? Gabriel thought.

"Someone we haven't heard from in a long time," Dad said. "They're a . . . a group, an organization. Enemies of the Nemos—I mean, I heard about them when I was a kid, and even met some when we went into . . . It doesn't matter. I thought they were gone."

"You have an enemy organization?" Misty said as she and Peter emerged from the door.

"Wait," Mr. Dorn said. "We can't have students . . ."

"Please," Gabriel said. "I need them."

"Yes," Dad said, ignoring them to answer Misty. "I thought we didn't anymore. But apparently we do. I have a . . . I have a slide presentation. It's a few years old, but I could share it with you."

Nerissa looked stunned. "Dad, Mom's been kidnapped, we don't need a slide show. What . . . ?" She looked at Gabriel, and he shrugged. *So, Dad's in shock and barely there. Great.*

There was a sudden, steady beeping from Dad's window. "Wait," he said. "I'm getting a message."

"Let's see it," Gabriel said.

"I'm sharing it with you," Dad said.

At first all Gabriel heard was a voice from a blank white screen.

GREETINGS TO THE NEMO FAMILY.
WE HAVE DR. YASMEEN NEMO.
LISTEN VERY CAREFULLY.

6

WE KNOW EVERYTHING ABOUT YOU.

The voice over the video was barely human. Whoever was speaking was pushing their voice through a device to change it into something deep and distorted. Gabriel stared as the field of white became the blue of the ocean, water splashing across the lens of a camera. The camera appeared to be floating on the surface off the side of one of the twin subs. Gabriel could see the other twin sub floating about fifty feet away. The latticework complex protruded from the water all around the two, connecting them and rising twenty feet in the air. Water poured off the connector. They had just surfaced.

THESE IMAGES ARE LIVE,
BROADCAST TO YOU FROM THE

EXTERIOR HULL OF THE
MAELSTROM SHIP *GEMINI*.

So it had a name. *Gemini.* A twin sub named after twin stars. *But what is the . . .*

DAVID NEMO, WE KNOW EVERY
DETAIL OF YOUR LIFE—AND YOUR
WIFE'S LIFE, FROM HER COMING TO
YOUR HOME UNTIL NOW.

WE REPEAT, THESE IMAGES
ARE LIVE.

Now the hatch on the *Gemini* opened, and two men emerged with Mom between them. She struggled against them as they brought her up onto the catwalk at the top of the sub. She stopped fighting. The two men and Mom were hard to see, silhouetted against the horizon.

WHAT HAPPENS NEXT IS UP TO YOU.

The screen now filled with a drawing of a sinking ship, its bow and masts sticking up through the waves.

WE ARE THE MAELSTROM.

WE WERE BORN OF THE CRIMES

OF NEMO. AND WE HAVE LEARNED
ALL THAT YOU COULD TEACH US
AND MORE.

Now Gabriel saw a swirl of images he couldn't keep track of, the video sweeping down the corridors of a busy submarine. Every crew member wore a silver tactical suit with a spiral and an *M* at the breast.

YOU HAVE TORMENTED THE SEAS
WITH ARROGANCE, WHILE WE
HAVE PROTECTED IT WITH OUR
WISDOM. YOU HAVE BRAINWASHED
THE GOVERNMENTS OF THE
WORLD WITH LIES ABOUT YOUR
BENEFICENCE.

That's nuts, Gabriel thought. *Governments barely trust us.*
The image changed back to the camera angle of Mom held by the two men on the surfaced sub.

WE DO NOT WISH TO RETAIN
YASMEEN NEMO. WE ARE
TAINTED BY THE PRESENCE

OF YOUR BLOOD. WE WILL NOT
KEEP HER.

Gabriel imagined the men pushing her off the side and closed his eyes briefly against the vision. *No no no, don't do it, don't do it.* But he had to watch the screen.

THERE IS ONE THING IN
YOUR POSSESSION THAT WE
WILL TAKE IN RETURN FOR HER:
THE DEVICE CALLED THE
DAKKAR'S EYE.

Gabriel looked at Nerissa's window in complete confusion. Her eyes were wet and angry as she listened. What in the world were the kidnappers talking about?

THE EYE MUST BE DELIVERED
BY YOU, DAVID NEMO. THIS
IS OUR NONNEGOTIABLE PRICE.

Now the screen filled with a drawing, an image of Captain Nemo, the original, Gabriel's ancestor. He was working in a lab, looking through a slit in a black iron wall. He had goggles over his eyes.

WE KNOW YOU ARE IN POSSESSION
OF THE GREATEST GIFT OF
CAPTAIN NEMO.

BRING US THE EYE AT MIDWAY
ISLAND. COME ALONE IN A
PERSONAL CRAFT. DO THIS, AND
WE WILL RETURN
YASMEEN NEMO TO YOU.

YOU HAVE ONE HUNDRED HOURS.

The image faded to Gabriel's mother again, a black silhouette surrounded by two captors, water lapping up over the camera. Then the screen faded again.

To a clock.

100:00:00

99:59:59

99:59:58

The screen went black.

7

99:59:56

"ONE HUNDRED HOURS!" Gabriel shouted. His mind raced. That meant . . . that meant they had to . . . He snapped his fingers.

Gabriel, Dad, and Nerissa all shouted exactly the same three words: "Mark the time!"

Gabriel's eyes swept the room for a clock.

"Ten twenty-three A.M.," Misty said.

"We need the timer back up," Nerissa said.

"On it," Mr. Dorn said, and then the numbers filled in a window between Nerissa and Dad.

99:59:50

99:59:49

99:59:48

"Okay, okay," Gabriel said. "Do you think . . ." He tried

to steady his thoughts. "Do you think they're telling the truth? That if we give them this thing they want—what was it?"

"That would be the Dakkar's Eye," Dad said.

"If we give it to them, do you think they're telling the truth that we'll get Mom back?"

"Don't count on it," Nerissa said. "We need to find them and mount a rescue right away. They have a head start from you, but they're in open ocean. We could find them if you got out here."

Suddenly Gabriel felt more grounded. Nerissa was arguing about the course of action, which meant they had choices. Because there were always choices. But it didn't mean she was right. The image of his mother, overpowered and trapped, overwhelmed him and he grappled to get his brain under control.

"*Maybe,*" Gabriel argued. "Or maybe these Maelstrom guys get rattled, and they shove her out of a torpedo tube."

"*Gabriel,*" Dad snapped.

"I'm sorry," Gabriel said. But he was picturing it just the same. "I want to go back to their demands. What... what's this thing, the 'Dakkar's Eye'?"

Gabriel was familiar with the name *Dakkar.* It was the original family name of Captain Nemo. In India, once, Captain Nemo had been known as Prince Dakkar.

"It's..." Dad scoffed, but there was no humor in it. He scoffed like he couldn't believe he was talking about it.

"They must have read about it in the data breach when they stole information from the rover."

"But what *is* it?" Nerissa said.

"It's a battery." Dad shrugged. "I mean, as far as I know. An amazing, unbelievable battery. A power source Captain Nemo was working on for years. It was going to be a gift to the world."

"Okay," Nerissa said. "So, whatever, it's an old experiment. I assume it's in the vaults? Can we get it?"

"That's the problem," Dad said. "It *was* to be a gift to the world. In fact, it was first to be a gift to the suffering poor people of Brazil. And that was where it was headed."

Dad paused as Gabriel leaned forward, as though he could commune with his father's thoughts through the screen. "Where it was *headed*," Gabriel repeated. He looked to Nerissa, then back at Misty and Peter. "Oh, no."

"That's just it." Dad nodded. "The Dakkar's Eye sank in 1910, aboard the Nemoship *Nautilus*, location unknown."

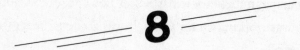

8

99:57:23

GABRIEL BRIEFLY FELT the room spin. A bunch of strange people had come in the most advanced submarine he'd ever seen and kidnapped his mother, and what they wanted was a rumored battery that no one even had? Or did they even... "Do they know that the *Nautilus* is *lost?*"

"My guess is they don't know it was on the *Nautilus* in the first place," Dad said.

"Where do they *think* the Dakkar's Eye is?" Gabriel asked.

"I have no idea," Dad said. "You have to assume they think we have it down here in a locker or on one of our bases or something."

That would make sense. There were countless treasures to be found at Nemolab alone, some of which even

Gabriel had never seen. Probably rumors of the Nemo vaults had been circulating for over a century.

"So...the task they're giving us is *harder* than they think it is." Gabriel looked back at his crew. "But that's all it is—it's just harder. It's not impossible."

"Do you hear yourself?" Nerissa shouted from her screen. "Gabriel, we are burning daylight. There is one path forward here, and it's to *catch* these guys. I need to hear everything you know about their ship."

"A rescue mission is too risky," Gabriel said. "Think about it, Nerissa. They could panic. And this is Mom you're risking."

"What do you think I even do out here?" Nerissa asked.

"I...you know what I'm saying." Gabriel tried to calm his words. "We could get her killed. The moment they see you coming."

"They'll *never* see me coming," she snarled.

"We have four days," Gabriel said. The time was ticking down even as they spoke.

Now Mr. Dorn spoke. "David?" He addressed the screen. "We've heard from Gabriel and Nerissa, but this is *your* family and *your* wife. What do you want to do?"

"We..." Dad looked down. His lips moved as he seemed to think through something. "Gabriel is...half right. We give it to them, or we...seem to. At Midway Island, they said. So that's what I'll do—I'll be there, at Midway, in one hundred hours."

"Okay then," Gabriel said.

"But we don't hand over the Eye," Dad continued. "They don't know what the Dakkar's Eye is any more than *we* do. So ... I'll make them something that we'll call the Eye. Look, all it has to be is good enough to fool them while we get Yasmeen ... *back*."

"You want to make a fake?" Nerissa asked.

"Now, it has to be a *good* fake," Dad said. "It will need to seem extremely powerful, even pass some kind of power test. I don't know. I can come up with something."

Gabriel glanced at Nerissa's face, then back at Dad's. He was acting calm, but this had to be driving him crazy. "Dad ..."

"I need to get to work," Dad said. "Mr. Dorn, keep an eye on the Institute. I'll contact you all when I have something."

Dad's image disappeared.

Gabriel asked Mr. Dorn, "Will you let me know if anything ..."

"You'll be the first to know if anything changes."

Gabriel nodded and walked out with Peter and Misty. They headed straight back to the *Obscure*.

"What's our readiness?" he asked once they were on the elevator.

Misty said, "It was a minor breach. One panel, so we got it sealed in minutes. They're swapping out the torpedo bay door, too. We're lucky; we only had one extra."

"Small favors." The elevator opened, and the three of them ran through the library and back to the hidden entrance. Within minutes they were entering the bridge once again. "We need another plan," Gabriel said into his headset as he put it on.

"You're telling me," Nerissa answered him from the intercom on the bridge as Peter powered up the *Obscure*'s engines.

"First off," Gabriel said, leaning back against a panel and shaking his head, "is it me or does Dad seem to be acting, like, strangely?"

"Yeah, let me show you a slide show I have on that," Nerissa said.

"It's . . . amazing," Gabriel said. "Okay. Options."

Misty asked, "So we're not just gonna let Dr. Nemo work his magic?"

"The magic of making a fake super-battery?" Peter responded. "Gabe's right; that can't be the only plan."

"We need to look for them," Nerissa said.

"Yeah. Okay," Gabriel said. "If you go looking for the twin sub, this *Gemini*," he said, "and you *do* find them, then I know you have a shot. You're the best there is. But don't be fooled. This is no regular sub, Nerissa. That ship is nearly half again as big as yours, and I think it's twice as armed. We barely escaped it."

"Noted," Nerissa said.

Gabriel wasn't finished. "And . . . on the off chance that

you can't find them, I need to get the kidnappers what they want."

"Ugh." Nerissa breathed heavily into the mic. "You're talking about a wild-goose chase. Not just *a* wild-goose chase—it's *the* wild-goose chase. It's practically the hunt for the Holy Grail. And I could use you out here."

"You have everything you need," Gabriel said. "And you also have everything *I* need. Didn't Mom give you a cache of information, everything there was to know about the location of the *Nautilus?*"

"Yes," she said. Nerissa had called it a *scavenger hunt*. Which was nicer than *wild-goose chase*, but not by much.

"Let's meet up. I need the storage device Mom gave you. And then…it's a race to save Mom. You'll run it by trying to find her," Gabriel said. "As for us—we're going to do it, Nerissa. We're gonna find the *Nautilus.*"

9

99:02:33

ON THE BRIDGE of the *Obscure*, Gabriel watched the sonar screen impatiently as the ocean swept by outside. He felt the weight of the clock ticking down as he looked at his wristband. "What'll happen when the Institute notices we're gone?" Misty asked. "We've been gone forty-five minutes already."

"They won't, for a while," Peter said. "I shut off the sensors to the docking door."

"And when they go to our rooms to check on us at some point?" she asked.

Gabriel sat in his chair and shrugged. "Tomorrow's Saturday, so that won't happen except for some random reason. We'll be long gone by then."

Misty didn't look satisfied. "We could have told Mr. Dorn, at least."

Gabriel said, "I know—"

"The deal is we're not secret anymore. Maybe from the other students, but the *Obscure* isn't a secret to our parents or to the Institute. That was the *point*." The point of joining the Institute, she meant. Before this, they had been working completely in secret while they all went to school on the mainland.

"I know, but if we had told Mr. Dorn, he might have tried to stop us."

"Because your father's plan doesn't involve us trying to find the Dakkar's Eye," Misty said. "I'm just saying that doesn't make me comfortable."

"I know," Gabriel said. "But it's my *mom* out there. We have to cover every base, and we can't get stuffed in our rooms for days on end."

"What if," Peter offered, "we all send messages when we're another hundred miles out. 'Emergency mission. Sorry.' Something like that. We'll be too far out for them to come after us."

Gabriel put his hands on his hips and looked up at Misty. "Good?"

"Yeah, okay," Misty said.

Gabriel nodded. He was thinking of the ransom message. "Do you think they know the location of Nemolab?"

"Your dad said they attacked a rover in the Valley of

the Lodgers," Misty said. "Nemolab is hidden about fifty miles from there. I mean, it's possible."

"But think," Peter said. "If they knew where Nemolab was, they would have attacked it."

"Maybe," Gabriel said. "But then maybe it would be easier to attack a rover if they just wanted information."

"But then, but then," Peter moaned. "You don't know. You can't know."

"It doesn't matter anyway," Misty said. "Don't think about the things you can't control."

She was right. Gabriel had to keep his eye on the mission. "How long till we reach the rendezvous point?" Nerissa was turning back east to meet them while they moved northwest. Luckily, she hadn't been more than six hundred miles away.

"Another hour," Peter said. Then he glanced at his screen and said, "Huh."

"What is it?"

Peter flicked his hand over his screen and sent the sonar to fill the main screen. A little green blip had entered the outer ring, pulsing every time the sonar hand swept around to light up anything big enough to be interesting. The blip was moving in at an angle, chasing after the *Obscure* steadily.

Gabriel felt adrenaline pulse through his shoulders. "Is that a torpedo?'

"Uh...no." Peter was listening with one earphone to his head. "At least it doesn't sound like one."

"How far away?"

"About two miles." That was too far to see with cameras through even the clearest water. "Should I increase?"

Gabriel thought. Increasing the sonar ping would help them identify the shape of the thing coming their way, but it would also make themselves more visible. He looked at Misty. "Yes. For one revolution only, then drop it back." She nodded her agreement.

"Open torpedo bay doors," Gabriel said. "Just in case." Misty echoed the command as Peter swept the sonar hand around the screen. A perfect circle showed itself—literally, the thing was shaped like a ball. Then it fell back to a small blip.

"If I didn't know better, I'd say we're being chased by a dense beach ball," Peter said. "It's about four feet wide, but heavy, that's how we picked it up."

"How fast?"

"Sixty knots," Peter said. "And it just came within a mile of us."

"Can we hear it?"

Peter made some adjustments on his screen and then flipped a switch, and the sound of the thing filled the bridge. It was whining and warbling mechanically. "I hear water … It's got propulsion, obviously."

Gabriel's dad's words shot back through his mind. "Dad said they were attacked by a Maelstrom drone."

"Yeah." Peter nodded.

"They must have been watching for a sub to leave the

Institute. If we were farther out to sea, I don't think they could find us."

"I hope not, because if they could, it would mean they could track us," Gabriel said. "No, I think it was left behind by the *Gemini*. But why?"

"To spy on us?" Misty offered. "Your dad said the last drone was an information sucker."

"I don't want to find out. Time, Peter?"

"Forty-five seconds."

"Evasive maneuvers, move off, let's see how it handles."

Peter shouted aye, and the bridge tilted as he started to steer the *Obscure* down and to the right. The ball was smoking its way through the water.

Gabriel turned to Misty. "Can you shoot that thing?"

"Can I hit a torpedo with a torpedo?" Misty asked quickly. "No way."

"Options?"

Misty bit her lip. "I can hit *near* it; I can arm a pincer torpedo to explode ten seconds out in its path. Maybe shake it up."

"Yeah, good," Gabriel said. "Do it." Misty was already tapping fast, setting the charge of the torpedo.

"Away," she shouted.

On the screen, a silvery missile swept out of the ship in a stream of bubbles. By now they could see the ball, a quarter mile away. It looked like a space satellite sailing toward them. It was curving in its path.

The torpedo burst in the water, and they felt the shock wave back to the ship. The ball was caught in the explosion, and Gabriel saw it pitch up and around before it emerged from the bubbles and began closing in.

"Wanna go again?" Misty called.

"Too close," Gabriel said. "Time to impact?"

"Forty seconds," Peter said.

"Dive and increase speed. What about countermeasures?"

"It's not a torpedo," Misty said. "It won't go for that."

"Dive and increase, aye," Peter said, and Gabriel held on to his chair as they pointed downward. But the sonar began to beep insistently.

"Too late," Peter called. "Brace!"

What if it's a bomb? Gabriel's mind raced. *What if it's a bomb and not a drone?* "Be ready to close off sections of the ship." He rattled off commands as they spun through his brain. "Misty and Peter, remember your first aid and be ready to find your emergency kits. Locate emergency rebreathers in your mind and be ready to find them—"

Wham. A metallic thud shuddered through the ship. They kept moving. If it was a bomb, it wasn't going off yet.

"Where is it?" Gabriel cried. "Did it bounce off? Level off and see if you can—"

"Found it." Peter brought another camera in view. "Topside, aft section."

On the screen, bathed in the yellow aura of one of the *Obscure*'s floodlights, something that looked like a silver spider perched on the shining plates of the hull. The ball's thick legs held on by way of thin, spindly fibers that appeared to have grabbed on to the most minute seams and rivets.

"Yeah, it's a spider drone," Peter said.

Water began to spin and bubble around the belly of the spider as the thing split open and a thick protuberance began to emerge and spin, working its way down toward the hull.

"Not good," Misty said. "If that thing breaches the hull, we'll flood."

It's worse than that, Gabriel thought. That drill would send in more fibers to seek out information on the ship. But Misty's concern was the more pressing in the moment. "Can we hit it with an electrical charge from the intruder net?"

The *Obscure*, like all Nemoships, was fitted with an intruder net, a device that would send an electrical charge over the entire hull. A holdover from the original *Nautilus*, it would send a shock to anyone who tried to sneak onboard or mess with the hull.

Peter said, "I . . . I've never used that. Where is it?" He started flipping through menus on his screen, searching.

Gabriel shrugged.

"Hang on—that's a weapon," Misty said. "Just a weird one." She found a menu on her screen. "I've got it. The drone's not alive, so I'm going to use full charge."

"When ready," Gabriel said, and Misty hit the button.

The *Obscure* shook as the water around them turned instantly to steam, yellow bolts of electricity flying around outside on the cameras. The electrical charge would have fried any living thing on the hull. But the bolts swept over and around the spider. When the charges disappeared, the spider remained. And now it was drilling into the hull.

"Okay," Gabriel said. "Okay."

"I think . . . ," Misty said.

"Yeah. We gotta get up there."

10

"PINCERS AND GRAPPLING hooks," Misty advised as she unlocked the door at the farthest aft end of the main corridor.

Gabriel hit the switch to start flooding the dive room of the *Obscure* as soon as he and Misty got in. The dive room, an oval compartment whose walls were lined with racks and lockers, was about a quarter of the size of the bridge. The pair moved fast, fluidly, the way teams that have been working together for a long time can when they're very lucky. Gabriel grabbed a pair of pincer rifles out of a locker and turned, tossing one to Misty, and she caught it just after throwing him a mask with a rebreather already attached.

Water was up around his calves as he brought the dive

mask over his face, then fitted the pen-sized rebreather over his mouth.

Misty spun and opened another locker, grabbing a pair of devices that looked like thick rubber bicycle handles, each with a spiky hook sticking from the end. She tossed one to him, and he clipped it to a loop on his belt just as he unclipped a pair of cable reels about the size of a large clam—and in fact, they were shaped like large clams—off a rack and tossed one to Misty. The reel had a carabiner on its side and another one attached to the line inside it. He clipped the reel to his belt next to the grappling hook.

Gabriel looked down past his feet to see the dive iris, an escape hatch at the bottom of the room, ripple with green light indicating it was unlocked. They couldn't open the dive iris until the room was full, otherwise seawater would explode into the empty areas of the room and likely bash them both against the ceiling.

"Hear me?" he asked, speaking into a mic on the rebreather. He slipped the pincer rifle over his shoulder.

"Loud and clear," Misty's voice came back in his earpiece.

"Copy," came Peter's voice.

The water was up to Gabriel's mask now, and then the room was full.

"All right, Peter, we're headed out."

"Better you than me."

The dive iris opened with a *thump* Gabriel could feel in

his dive shoes. He nodded to Misty and then stepped in, dropping instantly through the floor and below the sub. He immediately grabbed on to a handle next to the underside of the iris before the ocean swept him away.

Looking to make sure nothing was coming at him, Gabriel pulled the line from his waist and unreeled it, clipping the carabiner end to the handle. By then Misty was clipping hers, too.

"It's on top, right above you, more or less," Peter said. Gabriel copied back, and he and Misty started to swim, their reels unspooling but keeping them tethered to the ship.

The Pacific water was cool at 150 feet, but Gabriel had air rippling through his thin suit, shooting oxygen around his body and maintaining a constant livable pressure. It could get a lot colder and he'd feel no discomfort at all. As he and Misty swam up the side of the hull, past long slivers of mother-of-pearl-and-black plating, he heard the quiet thrum of the engines, right below his own breathing. Then as they reached the top, he heard the sound of the drill.

They hung on the side and poked their heads up. About twenty feet away, the spider drone was working away, a reddish glow coming from the tip of its drill. To Gabriel, it looked like the proboscis of some kind of insect, like a tick ready to suck and poison. Except this thing was out to suck information.

Misty floated next to him, pointing. "See the monofilament lines around the drill? If I had to guess, those are going to come into play once it punches through the hull. They'll grab on to cables inside the ship and try to find one that's carrying information."

"What do you think they're looking for? Information on the Dakkar's Eye?"

"Probably," Misty said. "Maybe they don't want to put all their trust in Dr. Nemo handing it over, and they're hoping to find out what we know."

"Okay, you're security. Say when."

"You aim for the center, I'll aim for the drill." Misty scuttled crablike over the hull and dropped to her belly, bringing her rifle over and aiming. Gabriel followed, and when they were both in position, she said, "One. Two. Three!"

They fired bursts of yellow energy, concentrated and whipping through the water until they reached the ball. It shuddered and moved to the side as the tendril of energy caught it. Misty stopped and fired again at the drill as Gabriel kept firing on the thing's ball body.

Suddenly the drill burst, the drill bit flying away. The ball danced, spinning its spider legs around. "We broke the drill!" Misty shouted. She immediately shifted to firing on the ball with Gabriel. "Maybe…"

Suddenly the spider drone began running toward them. It only had to go a few feet before it leapt. Misty was still firing, but her arcs went wide as it flew over her, landing on—no, around—Gabriel.

Gabriel gasped as the thing's metal legs slapped to the hull like a cage around his body. One of them hit his rifle, and as he let go of it, the rifle fell to pieces. He saw his own reflection in the drone's silver body. The creature had no face, but he swore it looked angry as it lifted one of its legs and slammed it down toward his face. Gabriel was shaking. Those claws could tear him apart, but even if they just snagged his suit, he could drown.

"Misty, shoot it."

"Trying," she said. "Don't let it stab you."

Gabriel twisted as the spiked claw of the spider drone's leg smashed to the hull next to him. It reared up the front leg on its other side, and he scrambled, avoiding the next plunging claw.

It hit again, barely missing his leg as he moved aside. Gabriel fumbled for his grappling hook. He didn't even unfasten the gun, just left it attached to his belt, aimed up and fired.

The hook caught the spider drone in the base of its proboscis, and it let go of the *Obscure*, flying up and away from the ship.

Misty shot the drone again, and it was blasted sideways, pulling Gabriel free of the hull with a lurch as it began to flee.

But he was still attached to the sub.

Gabriel's body was yanked through the water as the drone picked up speed. He could hear the reel at his waist spinning as the drone raced away, and he felt the tug of the other cable, the one tethering him to the ship. Soon the creature was going to outrun his line, and very likely it would pull his suit apart. And then the pressure would get to him. Gabriel tried to get the carabiner of the reel open, but it was tugging so hard at the loop on his belt that he couldn't dislodge the line. He had to be thirty yards away from the hull now, and he was going to run out of line at any moment.

"Cut your line, cut your line!" Misty shouted from her position on the hull of the *Obscure*.

"Trying," Gabriel said. He wrapped his finger through his belt loop, trying to twist the grappling gun out. Hopefully he could tear it free and let it go with the drone. But it wasn't working.

"Hang on," Misty called.

A pincer bolt, a segment of energy the size of his arm, sizzled fast past Gabriel's mask. If he weren't wearing his suit, it might have electrocuted him.

The arc of energy smacked into Gabriel's grappling hook on the underbelly of the drone, and Gabriel instantly felt the line to the drone go slack. He whipped in the water as the motion of the sub began to pull him back.

"Are you all right?" Misty asked.

"Oh, man, that was good shooting," he said, and he touched a button on the reel. It began to haul him in.

"Peter," Misty called. "We lost it."

"As soon as we're aboard," Gabriel added, "we need to dive deep and divert. We need to lose any more tails." And they needed to go faster. They had lost nearly a quarter of an hour and they had no time to spare.

11

96:12:16

"WE'RE APPROACHING THE rendezvous point," Peter said.

A blip appeared on the sonar screen, very near and closing—a long blip bigger than an *Ohio*-class submarine, the length of two football fields. Nerissa's voice came on the intercom. "*Obscure,* we are surfacing."

Minutes later—and Gabriel, unable to take his eyes from the dedicated countdown on the screen of his wristband, counted every one—the prow of the *Obscure* broke the surface and leveled off. Rain spattered against the cameras as the waves churned. Stabilizers kicked in all along the ship, steadying it in the storm.

Peter swiveled the outside cameras. The view swept

along, the waves dancing in the darkness and reflecting the exterior lights. And then there she was.

The *Nebula*, five hundred feet long and glimmering in the night, moved steadily, bringing its battering nose some one hundred yards off the *Obscure*'s starboard bow. Lights flickered as an unfolding walkway erupted from the nose of the *Nebula*, moving on small engines across the water. The extending walkway reminded Gabriel of a silvery serpent hungrily pouncing on the *Obscure*.

"I'm on my way." Gabriel scuttled up the ladder in the back of the *Obscure*'s bridge. He reached the top and opened it with his palm. Rain fell on his face as he climbed out onto the platform. He held on to the handrails, waves splashing up over the lightweight, rubber-soled swim shoes he regularly wore.

The extended walkway from the *Nebula* fastened itself to the prow of the *Obscure* a few yards away with a magnetic *clunk*, and a long pair of handrails erupted from the walkway's sides, snapping into place with a series of chittering metallic pops. Gabriel slid down the *Obscure*'s starboard bow, grabbed on to the *Nebula*'s walkway, and stepped out onto it. He looked up to see his sister as she emerged from the *Nebula*. They met in the middle.

Nerissa was wearing a black rain hat and held it in place against the whipping wind. She had to shout for Gabriel to hear her.

"Here," she called, reaching into her jacket with her other hand as she steadied herself with a wide stance. She produced a seashell about the size of her fist. Gabriel had seen it before—it was a hard drive, basically, and Mom had given it to Nerissa as a going-away present the last time they were together. It had everything the Nemos knew about the location of the *Nautilus*. Gabriel reached out for it, and his hand met Nerissa's, but she didn't let go.

"What's the problem?" He looked into her eyes, and for once her harshness had melted away. She implored him with wide eyes.

"It's a wild-goose chase, don't you see that?" Rain pelted her face. "These people have Mom. We need to find *her*."

"Have you made any progress?" Gabriel shouted, ignoring her rehash. It was settled.

"*Argh*. You're crazier than I am." She let him have the shell, and he pocketed it quickly. "The answer is *some*. My notes are there. But it'll take…"

"I'll do it." Gabriel meant it. A wave splashed against the catwalk, and they both had to grab on.

"I think you believe that." Nerissa looked back at the *Nebula*. "So, I guess that's it. I don't have to tell you not to waste any time. If you find yourself lost, Gabriel—quit. Come join the hunt. That's the best advice I can give you."

"They asked for the Dakkar's Eye," Gabriel said. "And they hold the cards."

She nodded and gestured for him to come close, and then she hugged him and patted him on the back. "Then I guess this is your mission," she said. "We should reconvene in the morning."

Gabriel wiped rain from his face and gestured with his head back toward California. "You should know, we were followed out of the Institute. The Maelstrom sent one of their drones. I think we've lost them now."

Nerissa took in the information and seemed to sort it wherever it needed to go. She shrugged. "Okay. We're submarines. We're supposed to be chased, and we're supposed to hide. Thanks for the heads-up."

Gabriel looked at his sister and felt the need to say something. "It's my fault," he said.

"What is, Gabriel?"

"If I hadn't begged Mom to start the Institute, she wouldn't have been there."

Nerissa reached out her hand and put it against the side of his face, and he felt warmth through the rain. "Mom makes her own decisions. And so does Dad. It isn't your fault." She bent slightly to meet his eyes. "I want you to believe me. Because we need be making good decisions now."

"But you don't even believe in what I'm doing."

"There's where you're wrong," she said. "We decided, and you're going to pursue this. I don't want you to think for a minute that you don't know how to. If it doesn't work, you'll join me. But you're not gonna think that again. It's not your fault."

He sniffled and breathed. "Okay."

Her wristband chirped. "Now, let's go, little brother." She hugged him once more, tousling his hair. Then she let him go and he jumped back to the *Obscure*'s prow as the walkway started to retract. He watched her recede with the walkway, straight and trim as she merged into shadow.

Gabriel scrambled back aboard the *Obscure*. As he reached the bridge, the *Nebula* dove and disappeared from the sonar screen.

"I got it," Gabriel called, holding up the shell.

"Boy, she didn't keep that very long," Peter said. "Where to?"

"Hold this position," Gabriel said. "Everyone into the library. Let's see what we have."

The library of the *Obscure* was Gabriel's ... well, his sister called it the Sanctum Sanctorum—the holy of holies. On a US Navy vessel, it would be called the ready room. It all amounted to the same thing—the place where the captain did his thinking. The library was patterned after images Gabriel had seen of the *Nautilus*. There was no pipe organ (Captain Nemo was said to have played the organ while he contemplated whatever went through the head of a guy who went around trying to rule the seas), but there were two giant windows that showed the water sweeping outside, with exterior lights that drew curious fish even now. There were bookshelves full of books—replicas, mostly, but a few real and very old, because sometimes Gabriel liked the feel and smell of old paper.

There was a grand old desk Gabriel had chosen from a collection of antique Nemo furniture while they were building the *Obscure*, and several settees, little couches you could lie on or read from with rich red cushions that matched the thick curtains around the windows. And a table, where the crew now sat with their tablets. They kept their attention divided between the tablets and a large screen behind the desk.

Misty tabbed through the files on her tablet while the screen in the library showed the pages as she moved. "There's not a lot here."

"I'm trying to understand how this is organized," Gabriel said. After a moment he found a summary of notes, started by Mom and recently appended by Nerissa.

Misty was still controlling the screen, so she opened the summary and started to read. "According to this," she reported as she scanned, "Captain Nemo was en route from Nemobase to Brazil. There's a note here about a worker rebellion that he was interested in supporting. That would have been a long trip, all the way down around the tip of South America and up. Was that the kind of thing he did?"

"Yes," Gabriel answered. "So what happened?"

"Looks like they never made it. There's a map here that

shows the route to Rio de Janeiro. Apparently, Nerissa did a scan of that area but didn't have a chance to go around again."

"What about the Dakkar's Eye?" Gabriel asked.

"Found it—well, I found something," Misty said. "There's a note here in the summary—DAKKAR/LAND. Meaning what, like it was on land?"

Gabriel sat back in the settee below the screen. "Land."

"What?" Peter asked.

"It's not land, not like *ground*. There was a guy, a crew member named Land, aboard the *Nautilus* during the whole adventure with Professor Arronax. Is there anything indexed to the name Land?"

"Ned Land..." Misty brought up the entry on Ned Land. The drawing showed a sailor in a Canadian uniform with a harpoon. "He returned to the United States after the *Nautilus* was nearly destroyed by the maelstrom—the storm, not the group. This is another Land—Mickey Land, Ned's nephew. Looks like he kept a journal. He made it out. He claimed to be the last survivor of the *Nautilus*."

"A journal?" Peter asked. "Do we have the journal in the files?"

"Nope," Misty said as she read. "Got a *Boston Herald* article about how people thought he was lying. Everyone had heard of the *Nautilus* and thought that it had sunk in the 1870s, so they took it as proof he couldn't have escaped a wreck of it in 1910. But get this—Land told the papers that they were carrying the Dakkar's Eye, a vital prize that he begged people to help him go look for."

"But the journal?" Gabriel asked. "Do we have it?"

"There's a note from your sister that she looked for it. And she gave up."

"So it's lost," Peter moaned.

"Not lost," Misty said. She hit a button and shared what she was reading to the screen.

LAND, MICKEY—JOURNAL

SEAMAN MICKEY LAND KEPT A JOURNAL. PRIVATE HOLDING, LAND SHIPPING, JAMAICA. REQUESTS TO EXAMINE REFUSED BY LAND FAMILY. DAMAGED IN FIRE——HALF OF ORIGINAL JOURNAL SURVIVES.

UPDATE: JOURNAL SOLD AT AUCTION AMONG NAUTICAL CURIOS OF LAND FAMILY TO CMDR. T. BOUTROS, USN.

"Sold at auction?" Gabriel asked. "Who is this Boutros guy?"

"That sounds familiar," Peter said.

Misty flipped to another screen. "I'm checking... Commander Theodore 'Teddy' Boutros, US Navy. Says he's an avid collector of, yeah, nautical antiques. He keeps his prized possessions in a glass display in the captain's quarters of his ship and moves it with him whenever he changes ships."

"Wait a minute." Gabriel tried to place the name. "Boutros. What ship is he on now?"

"You're not going to like this," Misty said. "The *Alaska*."

Gabriel winced as she brought up an image of the *Alaska*, a six-hundred-foot submarine he already knew well.

"Yeah, that hollow feeling," Peter said, "is because *that* is the ship that we happened to hit with EMP mines and cripple a few months ago." An EMP was an electromagnetic pulse. They had used the devices to knock out the submarine so they could get away. "What do you want to bet he holds a grudge?"

"I would." Gabriel sat back down, looking out the window as a shark passed by. Was it possible to get a journal out of the hands of the US Navy? "I wonder."

"*What* do you wonder?" Misty asked suspiciously.

Gabriel asked, "Where is the *Alaska* right now?"

Peter got up and walked out of the library, his footsteps echoing as he ran onto the bridge. After a moment he called out, "Middle of the Pacific."

"How far away?"

"Six hours," Peter said. "If we push it."

"All right." Gabriel nodded, and he and Misty went back to the bridge. "Set a course to intercept the USS *Alaska*."

"Gabriel, no," Misty said. "There's got to be something else."

"No, this is next," Gabriel insisted.

Misty grimaced. "Why would he give it to you?"

"I don't think he will," Gabriel answered. "If we ask, we'll be arrested, and we don't have time for that. You and I have some work to do. I'll start pulling schematics for the *Alaska*. See if you can try to find anything at all about the crew and matériel onboard."

Misty crossed her arms and rolled to her feet. "You've got to be kidding."

"You just said yourself that he's not gonna just give us the journal, and we need it." Gabriel shrugged. Like his sister had. *We're supposed to be chased and we're supposed to hide. It's all dangerous. It's what we do.* "We gotta figure out how to break into a nuclear submarine."

12

WHEN THEY WERE within twenty miles of the *Alaska*, Gabriel watched the sonar spin and saw for the first time the long blob on the screen that marked the ship they were looking for. They were twenty miles away from the *Alaska*. Close enough—maybe too close already for a ship that would be constantly scanning for threats.

"Kill active sonar," Gabriel said. "Run silent."

Peter said aye, and the sonar hand stopped sweeping as the screen went dark.

"Can we catch a current?" Gabriel whispered. It was the best idea they'd come up with on the way.

Peter scanned the ship. "Currents are goin' the wrong way," he said. "That's not gonna work."

"Then how do we get near it?"

Peter ran his fingers through his hair. "I don't know. If we run at even half power, they'll hear us."

Misty stepped away from her station and went to the screen. "What if…" She looked back. "Can we risk another few pings?"

"Can we avoid it?" Gabriel asked. "I don't want to tip them off that we're here."

"Don't you think we can risk it at twenty miles?" Misty answered. "I think I saw something, but I want to be sure."

"I think we'll be okay," Peter said.

"Go ahead." Gabriel trusted the crew to know their jobs—even if they were just after-school jobs.

Peter switched on the sonar. They heard nothing as Peter held his headphones to his ear. Onscreen, the images crackled into place again. The *Alaska* showed clearly, moving steadily from right to left and slightly away from them.

"There." Misty pointed as, here and there, minor groups of objects filled in. One of these groups, a milk spill of irregular blobs, was made up of many smaller objects. "What's this?" Misty asked, indicating the group. "It's not far from the *Alaska*—this is a pod of whales, isn't it?"

Peter made some adjustments and listened. "Yes. Blue whales."

"Can we hear them?"

Peter nodded, unplugging his headphones. The bridge filled with the sound of blue whale song, high-pitched and whining.

Gabriel smiled at Misty. "What are you thinking?"

"They're moving roughly parallel with the *Alaska*. Can we . . . sound like them?"

"Huh." Peter folded his arms. "Can we sound like a blue whale? Well, we sound, our engine sounds, like a rotor, a big propeller in a housing in the water. If you listen for it, it sounds like a drumming."

"I think I see where she's going," Gabriel said. "How could we change the pitch of the sound of our engine?"

"You could run it faster—a lot faster." Peter hit a button. "We could do that. We could also emit the sound of the whales. I just started recording the whale song. We could blast it out of the speakers. Mixed together, we would sound a little strange, but if we moved—"

"If we moved quick enough," Misty said, "we could get in with the whale pod. Just run with them. And then get close to the *Alaska*."

Gabriel thought for a moment. "Okay, I gotta admit, that's pretty good," he said. "All right, let's do it. You have enough tape?"

"Yes," Peter said.

"Start blasting." A moment later, they heard the whale song emanating outside, audible through the walls.

"Start the engines, maximum speed—set a course for the pod of whales."

"Maximum speed, aye," Peter said. The walls started to hum, and the ship began to move again.

"Kill sonar—guide by camera," Gabriel said, and as the sonar went blank and disappeared, the front screen filled with a camera view of the open ocean, inky dark because they were using no exterior lights.

After ten minutes, they saw the pod of whales heading westward.

"Cut engines and fall in right below the whale pod," Gabriel said, and the ship curved and dove. "Blast the engine every few moments just to keep moving. Otherwise—drift."

They slipped down below the pod and suddenly they were part of a procession many times longer and wider than them. Sleek, gray bodies of whales emerged from the top of the camera and swooped past. The sub trembled with every passing enormous whale, and here and there little ones darted among the others.

For a moment, they all fell silent and watched the whales. "Just look at them," Misty said. "For as long as they've been here, they've traveled the same paths, in the same enormous groups. If you were like a . . . giant celestial being and you drifted by the earth and saw it spinning, they would seem like a part of the ocean itself."

Peter cocked his head. "That's a very strange thought. Do you picture yourself as a 'giant celestial being' a lot?"

"Just some perspective," she said.

Peter snickered. "'My perspective is I like to think I'm a cosmic god.' Okay . . ." He looked down and back up. "We should be about five miles from the *Alaska*. If we judge by their position and bearing when we had them on sonar."

"That'll have to be close enough," Gabriel said.

"Last chance to just *ask* for the journal," Misty said.

"Noted." Gabriel stole a glance at the countdown on his wristband. "Let's get to the Katanas." Those were personal vehicles about the size of motor scooters, good for zipping around in the ocean. They kept a pair of them clamped to the underside of the *Obscure*. "Peter, you have the bridge. Misty? Time to run."

As they headed out the back hatch of the bridge into the corridor, Misty asked, "What do you think, pincer rifles?"

"I don't think so." Gabriel shook his head. "If we get in a situation where we'd want those, it's over." He had no desire to threaten anyone. They would have to do this with stealth.

They ran down the length of the *Obscure* through several hatches—through the passenger hold and the supply room to the dive room at the rear of the ship. Gabriel closed the hatch and started flooding the room. As the water rose fast, he and Misty went through their routine once more: lockers, spin, throw, lockers, spin, throw. "I know you don't like this. And it's really my problem. I'd completely understand..."

"Please." She put on her mask, tucking a few strands of bushy hair up into it. Gabriel adjusted his own mask as the water came over their heads. Now she spoke through the microphone in the rebreather, and her voice sounded in Gabriel's earpiece. "You need someone keeping you out of trouble."

"Too late for that." Gabriel grabbed a shell-shaped reel from the wall and hooked it to his belt. She gave him the thumbs-up sign when she was hooked up, too.

The dive iris flickered and opened, and they looked down into the dark water. Gabriel stepped off and fell through the floor, and in a moment, he was drifting under the hull of the ship, enveloped in cold blackness. It really was a huge difference when they didn't use the floodlights. Gabriel touched the side of his mask to turn on its LEDs, and a dim beam of light from around his face lit up the water. He swept the beam up to let it light up the underside of the *Obscure*, its black panels and mother-of-pearl stripes glowing in the gray. The *Obscure*, its engines off, was still moving and would soon leave them behind. Gabriel's line was still feeding out at his waist, but he thumbed a lever and the line stopped. His body jerked, and the ship began to pull him along.

Misty swam next to him, the lights around her mask casting a halo in the water. She stopped her own line, and they flowed with the ship, sweeping their lights along the underside until they reached a sort of cocoon-shaped housing stuck to the bottom of the hull. They couldn't just drag a pair of watercraft. Shapes like that caused loud disruptions in the water and also made a ship more visible on sonar. The cocoon that housed the Katanas was tapered so that it created very light resistance and made less noise.

Gabriel put his hand in a recess in the cocoon and felt for a small latch, then backed up in the water as the cocoon split open, both sides parting and clicking into place against the hull.

Hanging in front of them were navy-blue motorcycle-like personal craft.

Misty swam to one of the Katanas, touched the engine button on the handlebar, and it throbbed to life, water churning out the back end. Then she unfastened the bike and it dropped down. She climbed on and only then unhooked her tether from the ship.

Gabriel let his tether go as he climbed on the other bike and watched the two towlines slide back into the dive iris. The *Obscure* moved steadily above them, and he dove at the same time Misty did, heading westward, so that they were well away from the aft of the *Obscure* and it left them behind.

They rode for a moment underwater, watching the shadows of the *Obscure* and the pod of whales moving steadily away. "Okay, let's go meet the *Alaska*," Gabriel said.

He felt it before he saw it, a vibration in the water that was impossible to ignore. And then a faint ghost of a shape appeared in the distance, and as they got closer, the *Alaska* came into view—so large it was impossible to see the whole thing by the time they were able to make out the gray of its hull. It was like a train that kept coming and coming, moving from their right to their left as they slipped toward its port side.

"Easy does it," Gabriel said. "We're just a couple of tiny porpoises far from home." It was unlikely that the *Alaska* would detect two craft as small as his and Misty's Katanas, but the hair still tingled at the back of his neck under his suit.

The *Alaska* was patrolling the waters slowly. Soon they were right beside the submarine as it moved along, making its way.

"The lockout trunk should be forward about sixty feet on the starboard side," Misty said. They sped up and dove, moving under the great submarine and coming up the other side. Gabriel reached out his hand to run it along the smooth metal hull of the great submarine as he remembered the schematic that Peter had found for them in the Nemo database. There were openings in a submarine, but very few they could use. The hatch above, used for normal everyday comings and goings while docked, would probably open to one of the busiest areas of the ship. No way they could sneak through there. There was also a thirty-inch-wide tube for dumping compressed canisters of garbage, and twenty-two torpedo tubes. Both the garbage tube and the torpedo tubes would be closed until opened by machinery from inside, and even if you could get into one, they were dangerous, because at any time a torpedo could be loaded, or a canister of garbage shot out at deadly speed. But there was one other candidate: the lockout trunk, a hatch that divers from the sub used when they needed to go out. That was their chance.

"There." Gabriel pointed as a sealed door, subtly curved with the hull, came into view. By the time they reached it, Gabriel could see it was about half again his height and about four feet wide. They shot forward on the Katanas, then counted down.

"Three, two, *one*." Misty and Gabriel slapped padded magnetic cushions onto the hull of the ship. The cushions were there to the buffer the collision of the metal of the Katanas with the hull. The magnets made only a soft thump as they attached, and now they were riding along tethered to the sub. They cut their engines.

Gabriel unscrewed the end of his handlebar, and as it fed out a line, he immediately began shimmying back to the hatch. Misty followed about three feet behind him.

They scanned the door and found a recess for human hands—it was at Misty's head, so she gave the thumbs-up and grabbed on. They counted down. On one, she stopped.

"Are we sure it'll be flooded?" Misty asked. "If not, it'll cause an explosion."

"It's always flooded." The lockout trunk was like an airlock, full of water that the divers dropped into. "And if it weren't, you wouldn't be able to open it anyway, because the pressure would keep you from turning the handle."

She nodded and yanked on the handle, and it slid easily

around. The door began to open out like any door might. But it was heavy and needed them both. Gabriel grabbed the seam, and together they pulled it open wide. They let go of their tethers and swam into the flooded space beyond. They were inside now, floating in a small metal room barely lit by their headlamps.

"Should we leave the door open?" Gabriel wondered aloud. They had discussed it but had no idea if it would swing closed on its own.

"Shut it," Misty advised. "We don't know if they have sensors indicating it's open."

He agreed, nodded, and swam over to grab the circular hatch handle on the inside of the door. With a lot of effort and bracing his feet on a seam in the floor, he dragged the door shut.

They hung in the water for a moment, looking up. Gabriel could see shimmering light in a room above, but no movement. If there were people in the dive room, the mission would be over before it started. He didn't need to look at his wristwatch to feel time melting away. "No time like the present."

Gabriel and Misty kicked and surfaced a few yards above. They treaded water in a pool in the center of a large, oval room hung with diving equipment, giant pipes and tubes running along the ceiling. The whole place was silent. Each of them took out their rebreathers, basking in the fresher air.

Gabriel touched a button on the side of his mask, opening a channel to the *Obscure*.

"Peter," Gabriel whispered into the microphone at the bottom of his mask, "we are aboard the *Alaska*."

"Copy that," Peter came back. Gabriel nodded to Misty and saw that she was listening, too. "I'll try to stay just outside—"

The door to the dive room swung open, and Gabriel cut the mic, hearing Peter's distant voice go silent. Gabriel prayed he'd killed the radio soon enough as someone stepped inside.

13

89:07:35

THEY DIDN'T FREEZE. They knew better than to freeze. As a sailor in US Navy coveralls entered just a few feet away, Gabriel and Misty smoothly, instantly dropped back under the water. Gabriel didn't dare move to put his rebreather in—he held his breath, looking up through the water into the dim room. The sailor stepped around the corner of the pool, scanning the walls.

Misty was holding her breath, too, and she glanced from the air above to Gabriel and back. How long would they have? A minute, maybe. Gabriel hadn't taken a big breath when he dropped under the water, and he figured Misty hadn't, either.

The sailor had one hand up, idly running it across the equipment in the room, taking his time.

Gabriel felt his foot bump against the bottom of the pool, and he jerked his leg away.

Misty's eyes grew wide. For a moment, the sailor looked over his shoulder but didn't look down. He returned to his search.

Gabriel's air was turning acidic. Soon his lungs would be on fire. *Take it easy. Take it easy. Sometimes pain is telling you something vital. But sometimes it's just chemicals firing in your body. You know everything that's going on. So the pain is nothing. It is there, but right now it is not important.*

Misty slowly moved her arms, keeping herself situated at the middle depth. Her eyes blinked rapidly.

He looked back up as finally the sailor seemed to settle on a shelf and choose a wrench. He took it, shrugging, and turned around.

And then stopped. Gabriel bit his lips, his lungs beginning to burn for real now. *Come on!*

The sailor put the wrench back and grabbed a different one. He hefted it, nodded, and turned again. He opened the door and disappeared, closing it behind him.

Misty and Gabriel shot up to the surface, gasping for breath while, at the same time, trying to keep the noise down. Anyone could come in again at any moment. "We've got to get out of here," Gabriel whispered. They grabbed the edge of the pool and scrambled out.

Gabriel looked down. There was a puddle of water at their feet. Once they were gone, if someone came in, they'd see the puddle. He looked around. "Do you see anything we can use to wipe this up, like a mop?"

"Here." Misty hurried to the wall, pulling down a set of work coveralls that was hanging among several just like it. She tossed it to him, and he knelt, sweeping the water into the pool and soaking up the rest. He looked at the wet coveralls. "We should wear these." He hung the wet pair and took down two more, and they put them on over their wet suits. He found a pair of hats, and by the time they were at the door, they looked, at least at a distance, like crew members.

"What now?" Misty asked. "If that guy came in, there's got to be more."

"There are *hundreds* more," Gabriel agreed. "So remember the schematic—what's the quickest way to the golden path?"

On a submarine, there's the path everyone takes, the regular corridors and ladders, and there's a second set of paths just for the captain. A nuclear sub skipper had to be able to move all around the ship at a moment's notice. In smaller subs, this was accomplished through sheer courtesy—people just got out of the captain's way. On a ship like the *Alaska*, you had the golden path. Completely different, direct paths around the ship marked with a bright yellow stripe that only the captain was allowed to use. But there was only one captain. So they could brave the hallways and hope their disguises would keep them unnoticed, or they could take the golden path and avoid just one man.

Misty gestured directions as she seemed to remember the schematics. "Down this corridor, then there's a door at the end that opens up to the captain's ladder. Then we're in."

"Okay," he said. "You know the way, you lead."

She put her hand on the door. "Remember, any door you go through, don't open it slowly. Open every door like it's the most casual thing in the world."

Gabriel nodded. Misty had done a lot of reading about spying in her regular pursuit of—who knew what she was trying to become, but it involved an awful lot of disparate skills, from Chinese to, apparently, sneaking around—and one thing she'd said to him had struck him as remarkable. She told him that no one stops a guy carrying a clipboard, and if you don't have a clipboard, just walk like you know where you're going and you need to get there now. Because everyone pays attention to their own needs and their own work, and they don't spare much time to second-guess the people who pass them by.

They counted to three, then Misty opened the door and stepped into the corridor. She started walking, Gabriel falling in behind her. Sure enough, the door was at the end of the corridor. But then he saw a sailor coming their way.

Another set of footsteps behind them.

They couldn't head onto the golden path when someone was watching, so they needed the sailor behind them to pass them before they reached the door. Misty turned around, and Gabriel stopped as Misty gestured with her hands like she was explaining something. They kept the brims of their hats low as the submariner behind them stepped around without a word. The other one stepped around them in the other direction, and they started moving again. By the time they reached the end of the hall, it was clear, and Misty grabbed the lever and wasted no time in opening the door. She ducked into the stairwell, and Gabriel followed, closing the door behind him. The whole trip from the lockout trunk to the golden path had taken less than a minute.

The ladder was empty, a hollow tube not much wider than Gabriel himself, slick with thick gray paint on the walls and bars. He heard no sound except the soft hum of the submarine itself and his own breath. Misty started climbing, Gabriel behind her.

Although the sub was six hundred feet long, everything they needed could be found in the ops compartment, the two-hundred-foot-long forward where most of the submariners lived and worked.

They followed the path Misty had memorized. Up two levels, then through a door into an empty corridor. This time they opened the door gently and slowly to peek around. Only one man would be in these corridors, and there would be no explaining their presence. But Commander Boutros was nowhere in sight. Probably in the control room.

The corridor they stepped into was long and metal-paneled, and their feet echoed on the floor. They stopped at a door about halfway down. "The captain's quarters should be right across the hall," Misty whispered. They cracked the door...

Two crew members were walking in this new hall, and Gabriel and Misty shut the door and waited for the crew members to turn the corner. Then they poked out again.

Gabriel felt a surge of relief: In old movies he'd watched with his mom, the captain's personal berth would have guards in front of it. But that was the movies. The captain's quarters were right across from them and unguarded. A dull plastic plaque, CAPTAIN, marked the spot.

They went straight to the door, a matter of steps. Tried the handle. It was locked.

Gabriel looked around. The coast was clear. Misty pulled a pair of pins from the diving suit under her coveralls and went to work. Picking locks was one of her best tricks.

Gabriel heard sounds. Someone coming from around the corner. Two people, talking. They were going to get caught right there. "We need to hurry," he whispered.

"Really?" she scoffed as the lock clicked, and she opened the door. "You gotta have more faith."

They hustled through and swiftly, gently closed it behind them. Then they turned around to survey the captain's quarters.

The stateroom was barely bigger than Gabriel's library on the *Obscure*, about fifteen feet long and eight feet wide, with a desk and a bed and a table and a chair.

And a bookshelf, right in the back. On this bookshelf was a glass case.

It was an ocean lover's dream, someone's personal altar to the sea. Gabriel felt a moment of kinship with the captain of the *Alaska* as he drew closer, stepping around the edge of the tightly made bed to take in the contents of the glass case. Behind the sliding glass, he could see scrolls; a compass, no doubt of some historical significance; a fragment of an antique wooden steering wheel, blackened with age; a wooden tackle block from a sailing vessel; and a stack of books. All of them looked old.

Misty slid on a pair of gloves she drew from her pocket and touched the glass, sliding it aside. "Which one is it?" There were about six books.

"The journal should be oxblood, deep red," Gabriel said. "And half-burnt."

Misty found two books with oxblood spines, but only one was damaged. She held it out, turning it over. The back cover and many pages were torn away. "Would you like to do the honors?"

He took it and opened the front cover. *The Journal of Mickey Land.* Bingo. He stepped back as she replaced the other book and slid the glass case closed. He wasn't paying attention, though. He was staring at the book. He swore he could feel it vibrate in his hands.

"This is it," he said. If they had figured everything right, this burnt book would lead them to the one thing they needed to save Mom. Gabriel knew they should go right away, but…he had to look. He opened the journal and began to thumb through the pages. But all he saw was:

112169 45978 46773

50 90138 67173 673672 346

…and on and on. On every page but the title.

Could nothing. Ever. Be simple.

"Ugh," Gabriel said.

"What?"

"It's in code," Gabriel replied, resisting the urge to smash the journal to the ground. *It's in code? In code? We don't have time to mess with codes!* His mother was waiting. He looked at his wristband. He had less than ninety hours to go.

"It's okay." Misty put her hand on his shoulder as she looked at it. "Put it in the sleeve behind your back, and let's go. That code was probably common; we can solve it in no time once we're gone."

"Okay." He couldn't hide the fierce, crushing disappointment in his voice. "Okay, you're right." He dropped the coveralls from his shoulders, slid the book into a pocket on his back, and turned around so Misty could zip it shut, keeping it watertight.

"Don't worry, Gabriel. We've got this."

He turned around and pulled up his coveralls, touching his hat. "I believe you."

They were turning away from the bookcase and were

just passing the desk as the door of the captain's quarters opened and a sailor walked in.

The crewman stopped, his broad shoulders filling the doorway. He had a bottle of cleaner in one hand and a small electric vacuum under his other arm. Gabriel realized that he must be the steward, there to clean the room. All three of them froze for a moment as they stared at one another in shock.

"Okay…" Gabriel raised a hand.

The steward dropped everything he was holding, grabbed the whistle hanging at his neck, and started to blow.

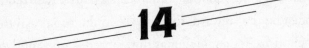

14

88:42:36

GABRIEL WAS ALREADY moving before the cleaning supplies hit the floor. Running forward, he dove into a slide. His feet smacked into the steward's shins and sent the man toppling. The steward tumbled to the ground as Misty came running up behind, leaping over him. They didn't look back, only heard the man's grunts as he hit the deck and shouted, "Hey!"

Misty slammed the door shut behind them as the steward blew his whistle again. They weren't lucky enough to be alone this time. There was a sailor coming from the right of the door, passing in front of the door that opened onto the golden path. The sailor heard the whistle and stopped. Gabriel stared as the man started to run down the hall. "We gotta find another way."

The crew member started chasing them instantly. Gabriel heard the captain's door open and the steward yell, "Sound the alarm—stowaways!"

Gabriel and Misty burst into the stairwell at the end of the hall. He grabbed the rails of the stairs and slid with his feet dangling in the air, down twelve feet. He bounced out of the way as Misty slid down behind him. Gabriel glanced up to see the steward making his way down. They went through another door and found themselves in another empty corridor, the yellow stripe indicating it as part of the golden path.

"Which way?" Gabriel asked, more thinking aloud than asking. His heart was pounding. They couldn't afford to get caught. He hesitated, pointing. "That way, then left."

"Right—correct," Misty said. They heard two things then: the sound of the steward reaching the floor above, where they'd come through before sliding down, and the distant ringing of Klaxons, reverberating through the ship. The door opened behind them.

Three more crew members in navy-blue uniforms turned the corner they were headed for. No good.

Gabriel saw a door coming up and burst through it as they left their plan of escape behind.

The new corridor was dark, lined with pipes and dripping with condensation. They didn't hesitate but just kept running. They skipped the first door they passed and took the second, which led to another ladder.

They shimmied down a yard or two and stopped, listening. Distant footsteps. Misty hung on to the rail above him and looked down, whispering, "What do you want to do?"

"It's gonna be tough to get back to the lockout trunk," Gabriel said. "We're already well forward of it." The door they had given up had been their best way back.

"I agree," she said.

"I have to admit," Gabriel said, "I don't really know where we are."

"What about Peter?"

Of course. Gabriel nodded. Keyed his mic. "*Obscure*, this is Gabriel."

"*Obscure*," Peter answered. "Are you on the way?"

Gabriel whispered as Peter's voice echoed in his earpiece. "We're still on the sub. We're gonna need some help. Do you still have the schematics of the *Alaska*?"

"Yes," Peter said. "What's up?"

"We're at . . ." Gabriel looked around him as he hung on the ladder. He looked up at Misty with a shrug.

"Wait, I got something," Misty whispered. She climbed a few rungs until she put her hand against a stenciled label on the inside of the ladder. "Aux 329, level D."

Peter exhaled, narrating. "Okay, okay. You're about seventy feet forward of the lockout trunk."

"Is there any other way out except the lockout trunk?"

Peter scoffed in Gabriel's ear. "Not unless you're hoping they surface, and you can sneak out the top."

"Okay, you'll have to guide us because we can't go the way we came."

Peter paused. "Man, the things you get up to. O . . . kay. Okay. I got it."

The door opened above them. "We're moving down," Misty said. "Tell us on the way."

"Good, descend three levels and enter the door marked level A," Peter said.

"Stop!" shouted a sailor above. Gabriel looked up past Misty and saw a man looking down at them. For a moment, Gabriel was afraid the guy had a gun, but then he remembered that only certain security personnel carried pistols on a nuclear sub. It was just too dangerous. But they might well run into such a person.

"Okay." Gabriel reached the door Peter had mentioned, Misty dropping next to him. They both straddled the ladder, standing on the thin platform that circled around it. "We're going through the door."

"Good, now hightail it ten yards or so until you see the third door on your left."

They were running, and Gabriel's voice rattled in his throat. "Okay."

"You're gonna step into a general passageway now," Peter said. "It'll be busy. Go left and follow the signs for the galley." The galley was an enormous kitchen that served everyone on the sub.

"What, *what*?" Misty said, urgency in her voice. "It'll be crawling."

"Do you want to get to the lockout trunk? This is how you get there," Peter said.

They put their backs to the door. Breathed. "We're gonna get caught," she said.

"Nope." Gabriel shook his head. He couldn't believe that. And he didn't.

Misty hissed, "Are you suddenly a head or two taller and a hundred pounds heavier? We can't slide under everybody."

Gabriel shook his head. They were going to get off this ship, and if it meant they had to go through a kitchen full of people, they would. *Think*.

His eyes rested on a fire extinguisher bolted to the wall. Misty followed his gaze and tilted her head for a moment. Then she yanked it from its clasps, hefting it in both arms.

"Can you pull the pin?"

Gabriel jerked the metal pin out of the top of the extinguisher, and Misty struggled to hold it, one hand on the handle, the body of it resting on her hip. She held up her free hand as she put her back against the door once again. Gabriel slapped her a high five. Time to go.

They burst through the door, Misty swinging the extinguisher out in front of her.

There had to be forty people in the hall, but they were lost in the cloud of carbon dioxide that Misty shot at them as they ran. They moved forward in a thick mist as sailors coughed and collided with one another.

Keep moving. Keep moving.

Into the galley. Gabriel took it in as they kept running, the carbon dioxide filling the air. He made out long stainless-steel counters and felt the heat of great steel cauldrons boiling. Galley stewards coughed, slipping out of the way as the CO_2 coated the floor. They ran on and punched through. Misty never stopped swinging, staying in front as Gabriel ran behind her. He leapt over a falling mop, and they hit the door in the back of the galley and poured through, slamming the door behind them.

"We're out of the galley," Misty shouted, coughing. She dropped the fire extinguisher, and it clanged away, nearly clipping Gabriel in the leg.

"Okay," Peter said, "when you reach the door at the end of the hall, go through it and down one level."

"Copy," Gabriel called. They got to the level and entered another corridor. Blessedly empty.

"Now, eight feet to your right, go through a hatch."

They followed his directions and found the hatch, stepping over the abyss onto a ladder. "Now?"

"Climb," Peter said. "Four levels. You've gone a long way down."

Gabriel agreed. They began to climb, Gabriel about a yard above Misty. He hoped Peter was right. His friend was having to use his imagination, walking them through a maze like something in a video game. *But what if they had missed something?* He gripped each rung and climbed as fast as he could.

They reached the fourth level up and heard a door swing open below. Gabriel looked down past Misty as she jerked back and did the same. A sailor was looking up and began to blow the whistle. "They've found us again," Gabriel said. "How much more?"

"You're on the fourth level up?"

"Yes," Gabriel said.

"Stop!" the sailor below said, climbing onto the ladder.

"Just step through," Peter said. "And look right."

Gabriel stepped through the door and Misty followed, and they saw the lockout trunk. Peter had led them to exactly where they needed to be. They hurried through the door into the dive room and found the empty pool. Behind them they heard their last pursuer come out into the hall.

They put on their rebreathers and dove headfirst.

"Where are they?" Someone's voice echoed from a speaker above the water as Gabriel and Misty pushed the door of the lockout trunk out to find empty, open sea.

Misty brought her Katana to life and hopped on, dropping and zipping back up next to Gabriel. Gabriel got on his own. He felt the journal at his back and said to Peter, "Switching channels. See you soon."

It took them an hour to reach the *Obscure*.

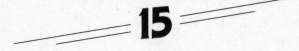

15

87:31:48

GABRIEL DROPPED THE journal down on the table in the library in triumph.

"Boom!" Peter shouted. "Off a nuclear submarine. Unbelievable!" He high-fived Gabriel. "Man, I wish we could tell someone about this."

"Yeah, don't do that," Misty said as she fell into a chair. "I need water."

Gabriel grabbed a couple of bottles out of the cooler next to the view screen and collapsed into his own chair. He slid one to Misty.

Peter clapped his hands. "Come on, let's see it." He snatched up the journal.

"Yeah, boom," Misty said. "You're up!"

"I'm up? I just walked you through a submarine, that doesn't count?" Peter took the book and opened it.

"What do you think?" Misty said.

Peter was taking in the numbers. "Yeah." He adjusted his glasses. "That's a little inconvenient."

"Can we decode it?" Gabriel asked. *Please tell me we can decode it.*

Peter sifted through the pages and shrugged. "You a master code breaker? Because I'm not. But sure, I guess. Actually ... hang on."

Peter brought up a screen on his tablet and mirrored it on the wall screen. "This code looks ... familiar. A lot of these codes used by sailors were not intended to be unbreakable, just ... you know, meant to make it more trouble than it's worth."

Peter scrolled through sections of text on the screen and held up the diary as he did.

Gabriel and Misty shrugged and rose to gather behind him, and Gabriel looked from the handwritten pages to the text on the screen.

"Is that the Nemo database?" Gabriel squinted. "I've never seen all of this." The crew had access to practically everything in the Nemo network systems, but most of what even Gabriel had studied was the stuff they used all the time— data on sea creatures, ocean pathways, weather. Even the biographical material they'd been looking at was new to him.

"A lot of databases have a list of codes, but yeah, this one is yours. Congrats. This is just an example. I'm gonna have to scan in some of the code and run a search. We'll be looking for *known* codes, the ones that have already been broken," Peter said. "If we can find one that matches, it'll go a lot easier."

"Easier how?" Gabriel asked.

"Well, then it would mean we have a key and it's just work, tedium, but it can get done."

"What if we can't find a match?"

"If we can't find a match?" Peter lowered the diary, looking back at Gabriel. "Then...then we'll..." He shrugged.

"Then we'll think of something else," Misty said, slapping Peter on the shoulder.

"Don't even think that," Gabriel said. He stretched his arms, feeling energy return to his body. "We pulled off a submarine heist. You're one of us. We can do anything."

Peter grinned. "I love the confidence, but..."

"No buts!" Gabriel pointed at Peter. "This is all you." He gestured at Misty. "Are we on course for Midway?" It was the only solid location they had.

"Set," Peter said.

"How long will it take to get there, if that's where we're going?"

"Forty-two or so more hours."

Gabriel looked at the countdown. "Okay. We have

about eighty-seven and a half hours to go. We need to start thinking about rest. Misty and I just ran a marathon . . . and you and I were up all night with the model," he remembered. "If we don't have the code cracked in, I don't know, three hours, we . . . rethink this." He sighed. He didn't want to rethink this.

Misty and Gabriel left Peter to his work and stepped onto the bridge of the *Obscure*. Gabriel turned to her. "You want to sleep. I'll take the first watch."

Misty leaned against her station. "I'll take it. You said yourself, you guys were up all night. Four hours, then you're on watch."

"Aye, aye," he said.

Gabriel went back to his quarters and dropped into his bunk, staring up at the shimmering interior of the curved roof. He opened the shutters and looked out at the particles visible in the waves as they passed by.

His own reflected face stared back. The nose that was so like his mother's. He saw her, saw images he didn't want to see, and forcefully shut his eyes, feeling his body spike with adrenaline as the terrible thoughts came in. His mom was being held. How in the world was he supposed to sleep? He couldn't. But he did.

Suddenly Gabriel awoke and looked at his wristband. A call signal was beeping on his nightstand. He slapped at it as he sat up. He felt guilty for sleeping, and at the same time guilty for feeling guilty. "Yes?"

"Sorry to wake you," Peter said. "But Gabriel, I got it. I got it!"

His crew. Amazing.

Peter stood near the screen in the library, which he had divided in half to display two pages of code. "Okay," he said. Then he glanced at Gabriel. "You okay? You look tired."

Gabriel waved his hand. But he felt his stomach grumble. "I'm okay. I'm hungry." He went to a small panel next to a seascape painting in the back of the library and pulled out a green smoothie in a biodegradable bottle. He grabbed an extra one for Misty before offering one to Peter.

"I'm good," Peter said.

Gabriel untwisted the cap and sipped the smoothie. His stomach settled instantly. "What do you have?"

Misty poked her head in and then took a seat. "We're clear for the next two hundred miles," she said. "I want to see, too." She took the smoothie Gabriel offered.

Peter said, "Well, first, I eliminated the codes that were invented since 1910 and that cut the searches in half. But there was still a problem—"

"Peter, just…" Gabriel shook his head. "I think it's amazing that you solved it, but for now, just jump to the end."

"It's a *Nemo code*." Peter laughed and clapped his hands.

"What?"

"It's one of *yours*, which, really, I thought it might be. It's a code that was used by sailors who worked with the

Nemos in the nineteenth century. Captain Nemo himself had his crew learn it. I mean, it's based on one of the ciphers from the South Pacific—never mind. The point is that we don't just have clues, we have a whole cipher."

"So we can decode it."

"Not *can*," Peter said with another laugh. "I already *have*." He tapped a key, and the right side of the screen went dark.

When it lit up again, Gabriel read:

OCTOBER 23

calm seas today, thank goodness, because we spent all day on the surface. captain Nemo . . .

"Oh, my," Gabriel said. "Peter, you're a genius."

"I have moments," he said. "You wanna read this thing?"

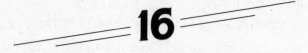

16

OCTOBER 24, 1910

For the past three days we have been steaming for Rio de Janeiro, there to meet up with the rebels that captain Nemo has felt such affinity for. i was there when he gathered us on the shore of Lincoln island and told us of the uprising that gave him such hope. ·

What a figure is the captain! When he speaks, everyone falls silent, and even in the wind and against the ocean, his voice strains not at all. He told us that the workers of Brazil, long abused, have begun a movement—not to overthrow their masters, no, but to demand treatment such as may become a man. This would be the mission of the *Nautilus*—to take to them a gift that would bring them power and with any luck might fund their new, more equal world.

That gift is the Dakkar's Eye, a silver device no bigger than a coconut; this i know because he displayed the small wooden casket in which the thing was kept. He explained that the Dakkar's Eye will power machines many times greater and more in number than the *Nautilus*, and he wants to give it to the world, allowing it first to be used by these men in Brazil.

That was all we needed—the word of the captain that we bore a great gift and are bound for worthy recipients.

i have seen little of the captain in the last two days, although i did observe him working in his laboratory aft. it was my duty to peek my head in and remind him of his luncheon, and i observed him before a small leaden wall about the height of his shoulders. He was looking through a slit in the lead while he worked his arms inside sleeves that i could barely see in holes in the lead wall.

Next to him, Umberto, his assistant on this trip, took notes as Nemo muttered things to him that i could not hear. Umberto is a pleasant sort, tall and young, with thick glasses, wearing a long heavy smock. He looks at every moment like a barber, the kind that may need to cut you open and would know how to do it.

Strange work, but such is the work of Nemo!

The kitchen calls me, and it is time to serve the crew.

OCTOBER 26, 1910

A strange day: Halfway through the night i was awakened to hear the screaming of men and rose from my bunk ready to do battle—but with what? When i looked out the nearest portal, i saw only the sea. No fool would attempt to board such a craft as this. So, then, what occurred to cause the screaming?

i ran toward the lab with two of my fellows and found the captain outside the lab door, his hair in disarray, shouting for everyone to stay back. The screams we heard were no more, but now i realized that the one i had heard had been Umberto.

The captain ordered the ship to surface, and so we rest and have gone about our regular duties waiting to hear from him.

OCTOBER 27, 1910

Stranger still. Today the captain pulled me aside for special work, because, he said, unlike my fellows, i had at least seen into the laboratory. When i followed him to the corridor outside the lab, he bade me put on a diving suit—heavier than any i have ever experienced. The helmet was thick, with special glass in only the narrowest slit near the eyes. The body of the suit was heavy, leaden, and indeed when i asked if it were lead in the suit, he said aye.

Clad in a suit identical to the one he had given me, the captain led me into his lab. It is not very large, about the size of our galley, and the lead wall I had observed before was the focus of the room. Captain Nemo led me to and around the little wall.

Behind it, seated at a table, was Umberto, dead, and this is all my Christian heart can bear to relate. Before him was the wooden casket that held the Dakkar's Eye. It was cracked, and I could see blue light seeping out of the cracks, the wood itself giving off streams of heat.

Captain Nemo bade me pick up a pair of tongs, and he did the same, and we lifted the wooden casket from the hands of the poor assistant and gingerly—gingerly, said the captain—nestled it into the lead box.

Captain Nemo pointed out to me a silver box on the shelf. It was larger than the wooden casket, and ornate, with engravings of the orient that I could not read. It had a hinged top that opened in two down the middle and was not fastened. At the captain's instruction, I laid this box on the table, and we used the tongs to lift the lead casket and drop this into the silver. Then with the tongs, the captain closed the two sides of the top of the box and turned the fastener, an ornamented lotus flower. He turned it once, twice, and again, and then, satisfied, stepped away.

Next the captain and i lifted from the ground a heavy lead box and set this on the table. And this we filled with the silver box, then shut the leaden one.

is this locked? asked i.

Nay, not locked, said he, just closed, but the silver box will take a minute to open— giving anyone who seeks to open it time to think whether they mean to or not.

A few flecks of paint fell on the table, and i looked up to see that the ceiling of the laboratory was burnt, a great stain spread across the paint on the metal there.

The captain retired to his library, there to think as the rest of us wait for further orders.

OCTOBER 28, 1910

Still no decision, but the crew is distracted, for several have taken ill.

OCTOBER 29, 1910

The captain has changed our orders, and we are not to go to Brazil but are bound for Gilbert ∨ important we arrive in three days.

NOVEMBER 2, 1910

Arrive Gilbert. Seven of my mates are abed, and their mysterious illness is impossible to understand. They swell like men stung; thirst cannot be sated.

NOVEMBER 3, 1910

A new pl—

There was no more. Beyond that, flecks of burnt paper. "That's it?" Gabriel turned back to the journal and picked it up. Indeed, the coded words ended suddenly. Beyond that were blank pages, long ago waterlogged and dried.

One of the pages broke in his hand, flecks of paper drifting to the floor.

Peter nodded. "But we know a lot."

"Yeah." Misty went to one of the large windows of the library and swept her hand over the glass in a large, curving *W* formation. The glass instantly went white and opaque. She looked back, and Peter tossed her a marker that he pulled off Gabriel's desk.

"So. First, the Dakkar's Eye. What do we know?"

Gabriel rattled off the way the sailor had described the device and Misty wrote:

ENCASED IN SILVER

BLOCKED WITH LEAD

"And there was a burn stain over the experiment," Misty said. "Meaning some energy escaped. And then…" She went quiet and wrote:

SICK CREW

SWELLING

"So," Peter said, "that kinda sounds like it was radioactive."

"Is that even possible?" Gabriel held up a hand. "You really think the *Nautilus* was carrying a nuclear experiment in 1910?"

"Absolutely," Misty said. "By 1910, Madame Curie had already won a Nobel Prize."

"I mean, the things you know," Peter said.

"So could that be why the *Nautilus* sank? A nuclear accident?" Gabriel asked. He rubbed his forehead. "If that were the case . . ."

"We'll leave it alone," Misty said. "We have Geiger counters. If we find it and it's radioactive, you have your answer."

"Yeah." Gabriel dropped into a chair.

"Hey," Peter said. "I want to know you're listening. Don't kid yourself. If it's deadly, you can't get it. We'd find it and mark it—"

"Because we found the *Nautilus*—" said Gabriel.

"Right. But you wouldn't be able to retrieve it. Like Misty says, we have Geiger counters. They'll tell us if there are dangerous levels of radiation."

"Okay, so . . ."

Misty turned around and wrote another word.

GILBERT

"Gilbert," Peter read. "The diary says . . ."

"Bound for Gilbert," Gabriel recalled. "And then *Arrive Gilbert*."

Peter propped his tablet on the table and tapped. "Gilbert. There are two. One is a small chain of islands and it's not called Gilbert anymore; it's Kiribati now. In the South Pacific. The other is a trench in Antarctica off the Weddell Sea."

Gabriel thought about the clock ticking away. "What are the odds they went to Antarctica?"

"It depends on how far they got. They were headed to Brazil, so they would have gotten down by Antarctica on the way. But if the calamity happened earlier, they would have stayed in the Pacific," Misty said. "And of course, what was true for them is true for us. We can reach the Gilbert Islands in the South Pacific in—what, Peter?"

"Forty-three hours."

"And the Antarctica spot?"

"Would take about one hundred and five hours," Peter answered. "We wouldn't have time for it even if it were right."

Gabriel studied the whiteboard and picked the journal up off the table, weighing it in his hand. "Gilbert Islands. Let's go."

17

42:36:01

SUNDAY EVENING, FORTY-THREE hours later, the *Obscure* pointed its nose at the surface of the ocean and rose steadily until it leveled off, sixty feet under water.

"Let's see it," Gabriel said into his headset as he ran up from the passenger compartment. He had been antsy for the last two days, his body a bundle of frazzled nerves. They had caught up on sleep, but now they were running short on time.

"There's a lot of activity," Peter said as Gabriel entered the bridge.

"What is it?" Gabriel grabbed two nectarines from a cooler next to the captain's chair and tossed one to Peter. Peter caught the fruit with one hand as he pushed up his glasses with the other. Gabriel followed Peter's eyes to the sonar screen.

"The large masses are the islands, though you can see our sonar labels them by the current name *Kiribati*, like I said. There are sixteen little islands that make up the Kiribati group called Gilbert. None of these islands are very big, but there's a lot of activity around the biggest one, the atoll Tabiteuea." An atoll was a ring-shaped island around a body of water.

"What do you mean, activity?"

He saw a large square mass off the southern coast of the atoll. Oil platform, most likely. A number of craft darted around the platform. So, it was a heavy drilling location now. That wasn't useful for understanding why the *Nautilus* would have headed this way when it was in trouble.

"Why would Nemo have come here?" Gabriel mumbled aloud.

"I've been thinking the same thing," Misty said.

"Well, I got a better question." Peter picked up a laser pointer and swept it around the squarish building in the water. Multiple smaller dots, midsize craft, were slowly moving around the platform. "Apparently Tabiteuea is a place where the locals do a lot of fishing. So I should see some small fishing boats. But who are *these* guys?"

"Slow your approach," Gabriel said. This didn't feel right. They were supposed to be following a clue to a nearly empty atoll, and he hadn't expected to encounter traffic. "Okay. So, who are they?"

"Deploying periscope," Misty said. A portion of the

screen opened as a camera came online and a manta-shaped disc shot out of a small housing on the side of the *Obscure*, floating upward. Gabriel watched the color of the water on the screen change from black to soft green until the light filtered brightly through the water, and finally they broke through. The camera flipped forward, and they could see now.

The Gilbert Islands looked like the very model of a South Pacific paradise, a tiny haven of volcanic hills and gorgeous green trees. Misty used a joystick to spin the camera around slowly until the platform came into sight.

The first thing they saw was not the platform but a fat, tall, white craft outfitted with countless antennae and cranes for moving equipment. A science vessel. The ship was moving swiftly out of camera range, but Misty shifted the camera briefly so that for a moment they caught the writing on the boat's prow.

USS ARTHUR LYMAN, it read.

"The US Navy is here? What in ...," Gabriel started as he noticed the American flag hanging from the floating platform. Here and there, naval officers walked purposefully along railings and into offices. The platform was a floating city, a command post for a small fleet.

"Okay, that makes no sense," Misty said. "We come to the Gilbert Islands, and they just happen to be here, too?"

"Could they have followed us?" Gabriel asked.

"They are already here," Peter pointed out.

"So, for some reason these guys decided to come to these islands on their own."

Misty turned the joystick, and they saw the first boat moving away and four others anchored at intervals around the immediate area.

"Why don't we listen?" Gabriel asked.

"Thinking the same thing." Peter fiddled with the controls on his screen. He held his headphones to his ear, then flipped the sound to the speakers. Instantly a cacophony of voices filled the bridge.

"Can we get a feed?" a woman was saying. "*Lyman* to Dive Team Seven, are you filming?"

"Copy, we are entering the fence," a man replied.

"Fence?" Misty repeated. "What would that mean?"

Gabriel wasn't sure and shrugged.

Another man spoke. "Tower, Engineering, we've been running the blowers for an hour. Recommend we stop so Dive Team can show us what we've got."

Gabriel turned to Peter. "What do we have on the *Arthur Lyman*?"

Peter tapped away. "*Lyman* was part of a carrier group on patrol in the North Pacific... Looks like they were redeployed here... ten hours ago."

"Any idea why?"

"There's a reference to salvage. I think they got wind of the Maelstrom looking for the Eye, and they're trying to get ahead of it," Peter said. The Nemotech databases kept tabs on navy ships, but the information was far from complete. "There's a file reference. Nothing I can open."

"Okay, let's see it," a man said on the radio.

"What's it called?" Gabriel asked urgently.

Peter looked up. "Operation DeepCap."

"Yes, let's see it," the woman on the radio from the *Lyman* said.

"Can you get that feed?"

"Watch the screen." Peter pointed, and the view screen filled with static. A row of numbers displayed as a line swept across the static. Once, and again.

"Can you..."

"Working on it."

Suddenly an image popped into view.

The first thing they saw was the nose of a submersible, a small submarine, a beam of light shining from the nose. They were watching the video from a camera mounted on the submersible's hull. Another diver in a one-person submersible swooped down from the right. Before them, just below them, the smaller submersible dropped over the edge of a latticework of metal in an enormous circle, a high fence that must run all the way to the ocean floor. Then the camera and the submersible they were "riding" on crossed the fence and began to drop, down and down.

Sea silt and mud were billowing like thick smoke, then began to clear, and the particles of mud showed yellowish as they descended. In the thick billows, Gabriel began to make out a shape. A shadow of something cigarlike with a long, tapered nose. He made out a cubelike structure sticking from the top.

The mud settled and the image cleared.

"Hoooooly mother," the woman from the *Arthur Lyman* said.

Gabriel felt himself stagger, and Misty gasped.

Protruding from the silt was the nose of a very old craft with an armored horn at the front and a square housing on the roof where the craft began to curve. The housing had rivets and glass windows caked in mud. The rest of the craft was buried.

"Is it possible?" Peter asked.

Gabriel didn't dare answer. But at the end of the nose, just below the windows, was a single letter in a swirl.

N.

18

"THEY'VE FOUND IT," Gabriel said. "I mean, I think. Look at it."

"Is that it?" Misty asked. "It's hard to tell."

"This is where we're supposed to look." He was trying to picture the whole of the ship, extrapolating from how much was exposed on the ocean floor. He had seen models of the *Nautilus* his whole life, but he had no idea how accurate they really were. "The pilothouse is different from what I thought." He looked back. "It's square—the one on the model was sort of pyramid shaped."

"If it *is* the *Nautilus*," Misty said, "and not some other ship . . . we have to warn them."

"Because of the Dakkar's Eye," Gabriel said. "Though

they've got to be working from the same diary we are... They must have digitized it."

"You can't assume." Misty shook her head. "If they send divers down and it's radioactive..."

"I'd like to switch out submersibles," the woman from the *Lyman* said. "Team Two, prepare to deploy."

"Ahead full," Gabriel said. "Hail them."

"Ahead full," Peter said. The ship was moving, water thundering against the body of the *Obscure*. "You can talk." The loudspeakers chirped.

"*Arthur Lyman*." Gabriel felt the *Obscure* picking up speed. "*Arthur Lyman*, this is Nemoship *Obscure*, do you copy?"

There was a flurry of voices on the radio. Someone sounded a horn. The radio crackled again. "Don't come any closer, *Obscure*. You are entering a naval operation."

"I'm here to warn you," Gabriel came back. "That ship could be dangerous."

"I advise you to stop your motion," she said.

"Slow to one third," Gabriel said. "I repeat..."

"It's been there for a hundred years," she said.

"If you've got the same data we have, you'll know that ship was carrying an experiment that may still be radioactive," Gabriel insisted.

"Based on what?" the woman answered.

"Stand by... Peter," Gabriel said, "can you send them a scan of the journal page that mentions the lead box?"

Peter flipped through screens of scans on his tablet and nodded. Gabriel heard the screen *whoosh*.

"There's only one reason they would have encased the experiment in lead, and it's because they were afraid it was dangerously radioactive."

The woman scoffed. "I'm waiting for this to make sense. If it's dangerous for us, it's gonna be dangerous for you."

"But it belongs to the Nemos. It's our responsibility," Gabriel said. "If it is radioactive, our Geiger counters will tell us. But if it's not...ma'am, it's family." He laid on a lot of earnestness with that last sentence.

Peter smirked. *What?*

Gabriel whispered, "I'm trying to suggest that if there are, you know, bodies aboard, we should have a right to see them first." He waggled his hands. "There won't be, not after a hundred years."

Misty shook her head. "There *might* be."

"Then...it's the truth." Gabriel tried not to think about it. He wanted the idea as an argument, not a creepy coming attraction in his brain. He'd never even *seen* a dead body.

"It's six hundred feet," the woman said. By which she meant, *It's too deep to dive.*

Not for us. "Oh, I've thought about that," Gabriel responded. "We have aboard a pair of deep-sea diving suits. Nemotech. If you look at your notes on the Nemos, you'll find a reference to them. We would very much like to go down and look at this ship." He glanced back at Peter and Misty.

"Ma'am," Gabriel went on, "we'll have to cross that fence you put up, which is why I'm asking. We can share the feed we send back to our ship. I'll have my navigator send you the passcode."

There was no answer. On the screen, a sailor on the prow of the *Lyman* was sweeping the surface with a pair of binoculars.

"We have a deadline," Gabriel said. "If you let us look, you can get your answers now. If you don't, assuming you don't have the same equipment, you'll have to wait." Gabriel thought. Of course they weren't in the kind of hurry he was.

After a moment, the woman came back. "All right. It's your ship. But this is still a naval operation, and right now I am forbidding you to remove anything from that vessel until the government of the United States releases it."

Gabriel looked back. "We don't have much choice."

Peter whispered, "How are you going to smuggle it out?"

"One thing at a time," Gabriel muttered, then called back to the captain of the *Lyman*. "Stand by. Our navigator will send you the feed, and we'll make the preparations."

Misty used her palm to open a large locker in the passenger compartment, and a rod extended out instantly with a pair of Nemotech deep-sea suits. They were deep blue and semirigid, with Nemoglass-windowed helmets and servos in the joints that made the whole thing almost hold its shape. "Oh, I love these things," she said, and Gabriel could tell she meant it.

They started pulling the suits over their regular uniforms, snug fits. Gabriel tugged the helmet forward, and it formed to the shape of his head. Then he swiveled a ring on his wrist and felt oxygen begin to flow as the whole thing came online.

Misty performed a skater's lunge, jumping to the side and dropping one knee as her other leg extended behind. The boots clapped the floor as she did so, and the servos in the joints hummed brightly. The suit was designed for walking under tremendous water pressure. "I feel like I weigh five pounds." Her voice sounded in his helmet. "Man, I want to walk on the moon in this."

"Never know." Gabriel stood on his toes, and the action in the heel joints of his boots shot him up several inches. "Gotta admit, Dad is good . . . Peter, could you prep the escape dinghy?" The escape dinghy was a small sub that carried two people—three if they were willing to be uncomfortable. It was there for exactly what it sounded like: escaping if everything went wrong. It had its own Nemotech engines, its own oxygen, sonar, everything they could need. They could cover the distance down to the sub quickly in the dinghy, then do their exploring in the dive suits.

"Copy."

They hurried forward and up a ladder, the suits making it feel like they were flying. Peter came back with, "Escape dinghy online" as they reached the wall of the starboard shoulder of the *Obscure*, and Gabriel used his glove to spring the lock. The door shot open, and they stepped into the compartment. The escape dinghy was black like the *Obscure*, suspended in its little room and just waiting for water to rush in so it could go out. Gabriel's and Misty's reflections in the curved Nemoglass around the dinghy grew as they moved toward the side door. They looked like astronauts.

Gabriel unlocked the side door and stepped back as it came up like a gull wing. "You want to drive?"

"Absolutely," she said, and Gabriel crawled over the driver's seat and a pair of joysticks, and dropped into the passenger side, bonking his head on the ceiling because the suit kept overcompensating for his muscles. Misty got in, and the door came down as soon as she put her thumb on the joystick. The engines of the dinghy started to throb. "Peter, we're going to flood the compartment."

"Aye, you have the dinghy con," Peter said, meaning Misty was now in complete control of the dinghy. Water began to stream in, and the craft began to lift. After a moment they were surrounded by the water, and the right and front panels of the compartment swung up and away.

"Here we go." Misty pulled back on the directional stick as she pushed forward the throttle. The dinghy swept out into the ocean, and they were free.

They traveled for several minutes, fishes flickering around them, until the hulls of the navy ships were visible above and below the fence.

Gabriel turned on a heads-up display using a tablet he unfastened from the dashboard in front of him. On the windshield, a smaller window showed the fencing. It was a great sort of barrel in the water, metal poles at intervals to form a circle some fifty feet wide. He couldn't see the bottom through the mesh.

"We're approaching the fence," Gabriel said.

"Copy," came back the captain of the *Lyman*.

They were coming in about twenty feet too low, and Misty pulled back so that they soared up toward the lip of the barrel. Then as they came across the top, she pitched the dinghy forward, and they looked down and saw the waiting buried sub.

19

42:11:23

GABRIEL STARED, WIDE-EYED, as though the ship-wreck growing closer could be made clearer, could give out more information if he just focused harder. The *Nautilus*, a ship lost over a century ago. Sought by his family for every generation since. And just maybe the solution that would free his mother. Right here. Maybe. If his luck could hold for just one more day.

"Breathe," Misty said. "If I don't hear you breathing, I get worried, and I gotta drive this thing."

She was right. He exhaled as they reached the bottom, sweeping the searchlight on the front of the dinghy toward the half-buried hulk. The ship was enormous—the part they could see sticking out of the mud was just about thirty feet in length, already half the size of the *Obscure*, but another several hundred feet would have to extend beyond.

They could make out several portholes in the side of the ship as Misty swept along the side and came around again toward the nose of the old sub. They swept past the *N* symbol, and Gabriel's heart did a flip.

The mud-smeared pilothouse just behind the prow of the ship dully reflected their lights. The pilothouse was a square about seven feet by seven feet, with windows all around. That would be where a crewman could look out and steer the ship if they needed to move carefully among other ships or obstacles. "There should be a hatch forward of the pilothouse." Gabriel pointed, and they swept along until Misty's beam lit up a long door with a swiveling lock. As they passed, Gabriel saw something that made his stomach ache. One of the windows was broken, water flowing freely in and out. The ship was flooded.

"Breach," Gabriel said. "One of the pilothouse windows is busted."

"More than a hundred years old," Misty said. "I'm setting down." They swiveled again. The searchlight swept along the fencing around them as the craft dropped down next to the old ship.

"Okay, flooding," Gabriel said, hurriedly finding the right controls on the tablet. Water began to fill the dinghy, and when it was done, he sprang the right-side door.

Gabriel swam out and dropped to the ocean floor, silt

and mud exploding up around his boots. He began to move as fast as he could for the ship, listening to the sound of his mechanical knees.

Misty caught up to him as he reached the hull and touched it. "Is it Nemo metal?"

"I can't tell." Gabriel looked around and found a small, curved handhold and grabbed on, finding another a few feet above. The scurried up the side of the ship until they were standing on the nose, Gabriel's foot next to the pilot-house.

The hatch was about the length and width of a normal door laid down, and Gabriel reached down to see if he could turn the inset handle, a curved hole about a foot wide. He reached his hand into the slot and had begun to feel for a handle when something bit him.

"Yahh!" Gabriel yanked his hand back. He wasn't hurt—the gloves were reinforced—but he had definitely felt something try to take his fingers off through the fabric. Gabriel pounded on the top of the handle, and a large red crab scuttled out, darting to the side and away.

"Are you all right?" Peter asked in his earpiece.

"I'm fine; it's a crab."

Misty scoffed. "It seems like somewhere someone taught us not to stick our fingers…"

"I know." Gabriel put his hand there again, wincing a little.

"Even I know that," Peter said.

"Yeah, yeah." Surely there was only room for one crab in there. He found a bar, the handle. He pulled.

Nothing. "I can't get the hatch open," Gabriel said.

"It's flooded, so there's no pressure to keep it from opening," Misty said. "It's probably just rusted shut."

"Nemotech doesn't rust," Gabriel said. "I mean . . . usually. But it could be locked from the inside." That didn't bode well for the crew, though. Had the ship gone down with all hands, no one—except the journal writer Mickey Land—even making it out the hatch? *Grandfather, what did you do?* Finally, he looked back at the pilothouse's broken window. It was wide enough. "We'll have to shimmy through the window."

Gabriel stepped to the pilothouse and kicked with his mechanical heel all around, loosening thick shards of glass that came loose in chunks. Finally the window was clear, and they knelt next to it. Misty turned on a lamp on her wrist.

A white shape burst forth, teeth gleaming, and Gabriel registered fins and jaws and called "Shark!" as he fell back. Misty rolled sideways as a six-foot tiger shark, its mottled spots sailing right past Gabriel's nose, whipped its way out of the window. Gabriel landed on his back, and he froze for a split second even as his father spoke in his mind, *Don't freeze; have a plan and use it.* He punched out and smacked the shark on its side, and it kept going, swimming away.

"Gyahhh!" Peter said in his ear.

"Tiger shark," Misty said.

"You say that like it won't eat you," Peter came back.

"It doesn't like the odds." Gabriel watched the shark go. Sharks were not inclined to fight with humans generally. Most times they will bite if they mistake you for something smaller, like when they see your foot dangling and think it might be a fish. "Anyway, I don't think it could bite through the suit. I don't think."

"Uh..." Misty got to her knees and shone her light toward the window.

"It's okay," Gabriel said. "Tiger sharks are loners; there probably won't be another one."

"I know that," she said evenly. "Marine biology." Her breathing was slowing.

"Unless it's mating season," Gabriel said aloud, although he wished he'd kept it to himself.

"Is it tiger shark mating season?"

"You're asking me?"

She scoffed, crawling back to the window to shine her light in. "Well, *I* thought you knew everything. I see...a bulkhead."

Gabriel looked in to see an empty area where the pilot would stand. There was a half-open door beyond. "Okay," he said. He swam forward, flipping as his body moved through the window and down, and when he came around and landed, his mind registered it as history. *Aboard the Nautilus.*

Misty dropped down behind him, and together they grabbed the open door. Its rivets were caked in mud and rust, and it took both of them and their augmented strength to scrape it along the floor.

Beyond the door was a large flooded room, all in shadow until they aimed their wrist lights, sweeping them around.

Gabriel saw dust flickering in the light, and chairs bolted to the floor. The chairs lined the room at intervals, each with a wooden switchboard before it, the wood a rotted ghost of itself.

They swept left to right, taking it in. They lit up a central pole with a hood and handles—where the captain would look through the periscope. And past, and then a shape loomed in the light and both of them gasped.

Seated in a chair, wearing an enormous diving suit with a giant shell-shaped breathing apparatus on his back, with his arms at the switchboard, was a man.

"Oh, man," Peter whispered in Gabriel's ear. "It's him, it's him, it's him."

"We don't know that," Gabriel said, frozen in place. *Move.* He took a step, the light bobbing and causing cascades of dust particles to blaze like a halo around the diving suit. His mind was already shooting through scenarios. *In a disastrous emergency the captain scuttles the* Nautilus. *Ushers everyone out and locks the hatch and brings it to its resting place of mud. And he remains, alone...perhaps dying already, surrounded by the ship he loved, the only thing he's loved since the loss of his wife and child.*

He was getting ahead of himself. He breathed. Stepped again across rusted deck plates.

"Gabriel, if it's your great-great-great grandfather, I... Do you want me to look first?" Misty was just behind him.

He turned to her, the lights on his helmet making little stripes across her face. "Let's go together."

They approached the chair slowly, as though the man might suddenly jerk to life, startled. Reached it. The man's gloved hand was resting on a console with his hand on a large switch.

Underneath it were written the words *NAUTILUS— POWER—MAIN.*

Gabriel began to lean forward as Misty went around to the other side, both of them craning their heads to look inside the helmet. Gabriel was prepared. *A skull. I'm going to see a skull. I'm going to see—*

The helmet was empty.

"Hunh." Gabriel expelled air, almost delirious. "It's empty. There's nothing here. Ha!" He was incredibly relieved. He stood up straight, clapping his hand on the shoulder of the suit. "But why would it be right here..."

The suit and the chair crumpled backward, the glove ripping away. The chair toppled over, its base ripping out of the floor in strips of rusted metal and wood.

167

They both gasped and then steadied themselves. "We're getting spooked." Gabriel moved his hand, and the light flashed across a ribbon of white sticking out of the sleeve of the suit. A strip with writing on it.

Gabriel knelt forward and reached for it, pulling it closer. The words were in French. They blared in his mind as he thrust it toward Misty to read.

Propriété de Altamont Productions

Por

20,000 leagues under the sea

"No. Way," Misty said.

Gabriel felt sick. He dropped to his knees, silt lifting in clouds. "*20,000 leagues*... No no no, no, this can't... We don't have *time* for this."

"What is it?" Peter shouted in his ear, and the captain of the *Lyman* shouted the same thing.

"It's a prop!" Gabriel cried. "It's a prop, this is all a... a model, for a movie." Gabriel had never watched a movie based on *Twenty Thousand Leagues Under the Sea*, Jules Verne's famous novel inspired by the writings of Professor Arronax about Gabriel's ancestor, Captain Nemo. Gabriel hadn't *wanted* to see the movies, convinced that he would be annoyed by everything that they got wrong—and now he was determined to *never* watch one. His voice dripped with disappointment as he read the name. "Altamont... Altamont Productions, *Twenty Thousand Leagues Under the Sea*."

Peter was typing far away. "Yes. Uh, sort of. Altamont was a French movie studio. They made a *Twenty Thousand Leagues Under the Sea*."

"When?" Misty asked, kicking the rusted metal.

"1929 . . . It was to be the most expensive version of the book, but it was a failure because no one wanted silent pictures the year it came out."

"The most expensive movie got an expensive prop," Gabriel spat. "That explains what it looks like. And the rust. The pilothouse is wrong, the metal is wrong, because it's not real; they didn't have the models."

He rose to his feet. "*Lyman*," he called, "I'm afraid you've wasted a perimeter fence." He shook his head, staring down at the husk of the diving suit. "Let's go."

20

41:56:19

MISTY PUT A comforting hand on Gabriel's shoulder and led him back to the escape dinghy. Gabriel couldn't bring himself to talk as she piloted them to the *Obscure* and they removed their suits. It wasn't until they were all the way to the bridge and Gabriel sat down in his chair that he was able to clear the lump in his throat enough to speak.

"Get us about sixty miles from here. I don't want the navy stumbling across us or vice versa again. Sixty miles north-northeast."

"Sixty miles north-northeast, setting course, aye," Peter echoed. "You got some kimbap in the fridge if you're hungry. I defrosted it."

Gabriel ran his fingers through his hair. The moment

Peter said *hungry*, his stomach grumbled and he acknowledged it dully. Gabriel found in his little cooler a foil package that was soft to the touch and opened it to find several rolls of seaweed around rice and seafood, a Korean dish he had come to love. But right now it was just food. "Thanks." He took a small hunk of kimbap and chewed it. The salt tasted fantastic, and the rice was perfect for his hunger.

"So what are we thinking? The real *Nautilus* was here, but it's long gone? Like it fell apart?" Peter offered.

Gabriel knew what his friend was doing. Trying to lift him up again, like rekindling a pilot light that's gone out. Not cheer him up—bring him back to thinking. Okay. "No. The *Nautilus* wouldn't have fallen apart, not yet."

Misty said, "I know Nemoships are strong..."

"It's not strength or lack of it," Gabriel said. "It's that a hundred years is just not that long. We find thousand-year-old ships all the time. We found *that* thing, and it's nearly as old."

"Why was the prop here at the Gilbert Islands?" Misty asked.

"Oh, yeah," Peter said. "I did a little research. The director was a Nemo nut. He said he had secret knowledge about the real *Nautilus* and was using it to give the people the best version ever. In other words..."

"He had the journal," Gabriel said. "And put his underwater prop at the Gilbert Islands."

"Lotta work for a massive failure," Peter said.

"Yeah." Gabriel was thinking that could describe him right about now.

"So." Misty nodded and held up her thumb and index finger. "Second possibility: If it hasn't crumbled, why isn't it here? Maybe the ship was swept away."

"Possible, but I don't think so," Gabriel said. "Even a hurricane wouldn't much disturb a submarine at the bottom of the ocean."

"Idea three," Peter offered. "The *Nautilus* exploded due to something about the Dakkar's Eye."

"Land's diary doesn't mention it exploding, unless he got out before it did," Misty said. "And we don't have the burnt half."

"Maybe. So, idea four," Gabriel said. "The diary lied. The ship didn't head for the Gilbert Islands."

They all sat at their stations and stared at the center of the bridge as though the proposition were a statue they could spin around and measure.

"Well," Gabriel said, moving his eyes from the space in the center of the bridge to his own hands, "I have to admit that might be the most likely scenario."

Peter sighed and tapped a few buttons, bringing the pages of the diary up on the screen. "Okay, what did it say? I want the actual words."

The sentence hung on the screen.

We are not to go to Brazil but are bound for Gilbert V important we arrive in three days.

"Where were they before?" Gabriel asked, turning back.

Peter reached into a leather bag next to his station and brought up the diary. "They had been in the South Pacific, headed for Brazil."

"And yet the journal says *bound for Gilbert*—which would mean turning and going a thousand miles north. Why would they do that?"

"Maybe Nemo had something he needed or wanted here, and it was worth the trip."

"Even if he was crippled?" Misty asked. "The ship, I mean?"

Gabriel nodded. The idea that the journal lied was looking more likely.

Gabriel read the line aloud. "*Bound for Gilbert V important we arrive in three days...*" He ran his fingers through his hair. "*Why* is it so important?"

"Either something outside, waiting for them, or inside, like time left for the engines to keep running."

"*V important,*" Peter said. "I mean, if they had to get somewhere before they exploded, that would be very important."

Gabriel closed his eyes and opened them, and started to read from another page at random. He was looking for numbers and symbols.

"We crossed the thirty-fifth = and now..." He touched his lip. "What is that equal sign?"

"Well, we know he's talking about the thirty-fifth parallel, the latitude," Misty said.

"So why not abbreviate it as *Lat?*"

"He has his own..." Gabriel stared at the page. "He has his own abbreviations. The equal sign means *parallel.* Gabriel looked down. "*V.*"

"So the letter *V* doesn't mean *very,*" Misty said.

Gabriel felt a jolt of adrenaline creep through his body.

"So what is it? Peter, scan through the whole thing, can you, show me every *V?*"

Peter started the scan and soon the image stopped on a different page.

We had a minor hubbub among the crew just as we passed Mariana V.

"Mariana V?" Misty asked.

"Mariana Trench," Peter said. "They crossed the Mariana Trench, and he called it Mariana V."

Gabriel clutched his forehead. "Oh, no no no. We were wrong. We were *wrong.* They *didn't* go to the Gilbert *Islands,* they went to the Gilbert *Trench.* And the clues were *right there.*"

"Yeah," Peter said. "And you can kick yourself as much as you like, but remember the other problem with the Gilbert Trench? It's in Antarctica. Gilbert Trench is over *seven thousand miles* away." Peter showed the map, with a long line running from their current position at Kiribati to their goal. "Down past the southern tip of South America, all the way to the bottom of the world. And our fastest time—our *fastest* time…"

"…is seventy knots," Misty said.

"And that's assuming the engines are running just fine," Gabriel offered. Which sometimes they weren't.

"So, the fastest we could get there is…" Peter looked up as if he were doing a long calculation.

"Eighty-seven and a half," Misty muttered.

"Eighty-seven and a half hours. And even if we performed a miracle and we could hit, say, eighty-seven knots, a *hundred miles an hour*"—Peter dropped his voice—"then it would still take *seventy-two hours*."

"And we don't have it." Gabriel looked at the clock on the wall. "We have less than *forty-two* hours, *gyahhh*!" He slammed his hands against the railing that ran along the bank of stations under the main screen. "We know the right place now. We *know* it."

"It's okay," Misty said. "We'll…"

Gabriel bit his lip. Every time he blinked, he saw his mother. "It's *not* okay. What looks okay about this to you? A band of techno-pirates or whatever they are has my mother, and what I need is over seven thousand miles away."

"Gabriel, you asked me to keep you on track, and this

is me doing that. Now stop; stop and think." Misty pushed back her hair, huffing. "I think it's time to call your sister. We can pick up the search after."

"Don't you remember what her plan was? A rescue mission, and barring that, my dad's plan of trying to hand over a fake. No, I'm not giving up," Gabriel responded. "I don't know, maybe we could contact the Maelstrom, negotiate…"

"Wait a minute," Peter said.

Gabriel looked back. "What's that?"

Peter bent forward in his seat, staring at his own steepled fingers through thick glasses. "Okay, this might sound absurd, but…"

"Please," Misty said.

Peter slid out of his seat and paced for a moment. "It's, uh…Have either of you ever heard of supercavitation?"

Misty looked at Gabriel and then back at Peter. "I know bells are supposed to be ringing, but honestly I got nothin'."

"What, that's a Chinese thing. Right?" Gabriel was searching his memory. It wasn't something the Nemos had experimented with.

"Okay." Peter waved his arms, and it had the effect of looking like he was ordering them all to wipe clean the whiteboard in their minds. "An airplane can go about six hundred miles an hour, but a typical submarine goes about sixty. Why that difference? Why are submarines so much slower?"

"Well, drag," Misty said. "Water is harder to move through than air."

"Right!" Peter walked over to Misty, his hand tilted as he moved it along like he was pushing something heavy. "You're *pushing* water along. We try our best to make the sub as smooth as we can, to cut the drag in the water, but still. Water is heavy, and it's hitting the sub and pushing it back. We have enormously powerful engines just to hit a speed of about a tenth what a plane can do."

"Okay," Misty said. Gabriel sat down, watching Peter and listening intently. He loved seeing a brain at work.

"Okay!" Peter went on. "So, the idea of supercavitation is, *what if you put a sky around the submarine?* As in a big bubble of air that allows the sub to *fly* underwater."

"The sub keeps moving." Gabriel pictured it. "If the bubble keeps moving, the water flows around the bubble, and the cavity of air in the back keeps pushing you faster forward."

"And no water pushes back on the sub. It hits the bubble, which just slides on," Peter explained. "If you can do that, if you can make an air cavity around your sub, your sub could go as fast as a plane."

Please let this be going somewhere real. "Okay," Gabriel said, "but we don't *have* that. You're talking about something that would have to be an entirely new engine design, or at least a new body design."

Peter turned, throwing the same hand out, still tilted,

but now it meant *stop*. "Gabe, do you want to get there or not? Think about what you usually say to us. 'Options?' Don't think about *can't*; think about *how*." Peter spun around, this time gesturing *come on*. "Options. How do we make one? Right now."

"We..."

"Don't say *can't*," Peter said. "I told you. I've been with you long enough to know that if you weren't so worried, you'd be the first to push us to say *how*. *So come on. How?*"

Maybe Peter was right. Maybe Gabriel was so scared for his mother he was forgetting to use his brain. Okay. *Think*. "Make a bubble," Gabriel said. "How?"

"Force air out of the sub?" Misty said. "If you could force enough air out to make a bubble big enough for the whole sub." She snapped her fingers. "What about the tubes—you could use the forward torpedo tubes."

Peter nodded. "Okay, but it would have to be a constant flow of air."

Gabriel jumped up, pointing at the ceiling. "We already make a constant flow. The air processors convert the CO_2 into breathable air."

"CO_2, O_2, it won't matter for the bubble," Peter said.

"But then you raise a *real* problem," Misty said. "Which is: What are we supposed to brea—"

"Don't go there yet," Peter said. "Follow the thought."

"Right," Gabriel said. "Work the problem." Because that was always the way.

Peter was spinning slowly as he talked, and for a moment he looked like he was in command of the bridge. "Stay on this. Can we, could we *really*, use the torpedo tubes to force out a constant stream of air, ongoing, as long as we're underway?"

"Yes, until we overtake the supply of air," Gabriel said. "But how would you hold the bubble together?"

"Ah," said Peter. "We have what most subs don't: We have the electric shield, the one we use to zap intruders. I think... *I think*... that if we run it constantly, it will react with the air and the water to keep a constant bubble."

"Okay," Misty said, "let's say that's true. What about when you overtake the oxygen supply completely? Then we'd have to surface." Misty shook her head. "But anyway, there's *still* the little matter of..."

"Not yet," Peter said. "Not that part yet. Stay with me on this. Say we do all that, how much time would we have in the air pocket *before* we had to surface? Wait, wait." Peter had that answer himself. He kept his *wait* gesture up as he flipped through screens, looking for oxygen outputs, apparently. He tapped some numbers into a notepad app and gestured to Misty. "How does this look to you?"

Misty went over and looked at the figures Peter had put down and nodded.

"We would run out of air and have to surface in thirteen hours," Peter said to Gabriel. "Now, we don't even know how fast it would go."

Gabriel looked back at the map, and the line showing seven thousand miles to cover. *Could it . . .*

"Okay," Peter said to Misty. "Now for your other problem."

"Yeah, well . . . ," Misty said. "We're *mammals*, and we have to *breathe*. If we push all our oxygen out, there won't be any left for us."

Gabriel shook his head. "Aren't you glad you transferred to a new school?"

"No, no, we *have* air to breathe." Peter snapped his fingers. "Come on, guys, I don't even *dive*, and I know this."

Misty's eyes went wide. "We can use diving suits. Scuba gear. We have plenty of oxygen; the air in the ship will be toxic, but we'll just pretend we're diving."

"No. That's not a bad idea," Gabriel said, "but I can do you one better. We'll travel in the escape dinghy. It has its *own* air processors. Totally separate."

"So . . ." Peter seemed to be picturing it. "We abandon the body of the *Obscure* and control it by remote from the escape dinghy. Are there three seats in that thing?"

"Eh, the rear seat folds down, but it'll work," Misty said. There were two front seats in the dinghy, plus a cramped third behind those.

"Shotgun," Peter said.

Amazing. If Peter was right, they could cover the distance in a tenth of the time. *If, if, if.* But Gabriel knew Peter, and he put a lot of faith in Peter's *ifs.*

180

"Okay, let's do it." Gabriel looked at his wristband. "Misty, can you join me below? We gotta rip out the oxygen lines and shove them into the torpedo tubes. Peter?"

"Aye."

He pointed. "You are some kinda freaking genius."

Peter collapsed into his seat. "I coulda told you that."

"Keep telling us." Gabriel started walking toward the back. "Prep the oxygen processors to be our main output. We're gonna use the torpedo tubes as an air outlet, so you may as well take the weapons systems offline. Kill *everything*. All power to the air and the engines. Okay, is it decided?"

"It's my idea," Peter said, "so *yeah*."

"Absolutely," Misty said.

Gabriel looked at his wristband and said, "Let's get the work done—and us in the escape dinghy—in one hour."

"Sure, why not," Peter said, "because if we're gonna make an experimental craft out of our *only working one*, we might as well hurry."

~~~

"I hope we don't need these." Misty crouched next to a padded composite crate that held the torpedo they had just removed from the tube. The crate was used for moving anything explosive onto the ship. It lay next to three others—all the torpedoes they were carrying.

Gabriel barely heard her, because he was inside a crawl space nearby with a flashlight in his mouth, shifting large tubes aside, looking for the right one. He glanced down past his feet into the torpedo room where Misty clasped the crate shut with a series of metallic snaps. "I'm just gonna hope we won't." Gabriel looked back up and moved a large blue tube aside. He finally spotted a large hose the size of his head labeled O_2. "Found it."

Misty stuck her head into the crawl space. "You need the clamps?"

"Yes." She slid a pair of constricting clamps, metallic rings with machinery at the center, to him, and he grabbed them when they reached his knee. He laid one down and opened the other over his face, sliding it around the oxygen tube. "Peter, I'm cutting the tube."

"Copy."

Gabriel fastened the ring and then the next one, about six inches down from that. Then he pressed a button on the side of the handles, and the clamps began to constrict, tightening around the oxygen tube. The tube rattled and bobbed over his head as it thinned out where the clamps were, like a long balloon rapidly squeezed in the center. Then he took a knife and began to cut.

A moment later, Gabriel shimmied out of the crawl space, dragging one end of the tube with him. The end he had cut looked like the ruffled collar on a Tootsie Roll, and the tube of oxygen danced in his hand.

He stood up, looking at the torpedo tubes. They were

two tunnels in the wall of the torpedo room, each about a foot and a half wide, about six feet apart. The apparatus to hold the torpedoes slid out and back, so the entrance was fairly smooth.

"What did you come up with for a connector?" he asked. They needed something that could connect the tube in his hands to the two holes in the wall.

Misty turned around and indicated the thing at her feet. "Well, I took a pair of old diving suits and cut them open, then I welded them together and used the sleeves and legs as material just to make them bigger. It's a... pretty serviceable rubber funnel." She picked it up, and Gabriel grabbed one end with his free hand as the air hose bounced.

"This is nice," Gabriel said. The collar of one of the suits would fit the hose almost perfectly, as it opened to a funnel of fused rubber. He could still make out the original sleeves and legs.

They clamped the collar of the suit to the oxygen tube and then used a quick-setting glue—*do not get this on your hands*, he remembered his sister telling him the first time he saw it—and sealed the funnel to the wall.

They stepped back and regarded their work. There would be no test. "Okay, Peter, I'm gonna open the oxygen hose and start venting air out of the tubes. You ready to increase production?"

Peter paused. "Yes, we'll be pumping approximately eighteen times the amount of oxygen through the system as we normally do, and three times as fast. Uh, I recommend we do that by remote once we're in the dinghy."

Gabriel looked at Misty. "We, uh, we just might destroy the oxygen system."

"I know," Misty said. "I'm sorry."

"I mean, we won't die," Gabriel said. "We'd just go to the surface and ... and I guess chug toward Midway." And then all this would be for nothing, because they would have no ransom, and they would be too late.

"I'm assuming we got it right," Misty said.

He sighed and nodded. He was committed to this course. It would work or it wouldn't, but they'd spent ten minutes inspecting the system to see if there were any weak spots, so it would be fine.

Right?

I'm sorry, he thought, looking at the ship. *I'm sorry for having to do this.*

"You ready?' Gabriel asked Misty.

"Go."

"Okay, unclamping now." Gabriel reached over to the end of the funnel, feeling for the clamp around the end of the oxygen tube. It was clumsy going because he was feeling through thick rubber, but he knew what he was looking for. He found a thumb latch and fumbled his way to flipping it.

Air began hissing out of the hose and filling the funnel, which grew immediately, a little tent perched on the wall, its mouth over the tubes.

"Okay, Peter, we're now ready to vent our air. Meet you at the dinghy."

"Copy, powering down all systems but engines and air. Meet you there."

The pulsing in the walls, usually almost imperceptible, ceased, and the lights dimmed to an emergency red. Misty looked up at the ceiling. "Oh, boy, I hate when it looks like this."

"What, those aren't the best times?" They started running out of the torpedo room and up the ladder, and then met Peter in the corridor coming out of the bridge. He was carrying his backpack, and it looked stuffed.

"What's all that?"

"A surprise," Peter said.

They moved down the central corridor, past the personnel carrier room, the only sounds their footsteps and the rattle of the air tubes in the walls. They went through a portal in the starboard wall into the small room with a handprint on the wall, and Peter did the honors of putting his hand on it because he got there first. The wall sprang up, and they were looking once again at the escape dinghy. It was barely big enough for three people. Peter unlocked it, and the doors sprang up, and they climbed in.

Misty got in the driver's seat. As Navs it would have

made sense this time for Peter to take it, but he had to drive the *Obscure*, and this dinghy wasn't going anywhere. She wouldn't be using the joysticks at all. Peter hopped into the right front seat—he had called shotgun. He stuffed his backpack next to his feet and grabbed a tablet off a clasp on the dash while Gabriel climbed into the back. He wanted to be able to see the whole dash.

Gabriel reached over and hit a button, and the wall closed around them, and then he closed the window of the dinghy.

Now they were closed into the small craft in what amounted to a tiny pocket on the side of the *Obscure*. Misty powered it on, and they heard the hum of the engine as it rested in its harness, air-conditioning kicking in and sending air around them.

"All right," Gabriel said. "Oxygen increase?"

Peter brought up a remote version of his entire Navs station, and Gabriel saw a diagram of the *Obscure* over Peter's shoulder. Air flow was indicated by a bright blue series of arteries running toward the front. He slid an indicator far to the right.

"Increasing," he said.

Presently they felt the cradle of the dinghy begin to rock. The ship was vibrating in the water. If any subs were looking for them, they would surely be visible now.

"Energy shield?"

"Energy shield...on maximum."

"Vent the air," Gabriel said, and Peter said aye, and he brought up a view of the front cameras of the *Obscure*. Air began to force itself out of the ship, a cloud of dissolute bubbles. The bubbles burst and hissed steam as the electricity hit them and the oxygen flowed over, dissipating. He increased the air flow again.

"Moving to flank speed," Peter said, and the ship slowly moved forward.

"Increase to maximum air," Gabriel said, and the ship began to vibrate more fully as the bubbles increased, the steam bursting, and suddenly they could see the wet surface of the ship moment to moment inside the bubbles. Larger bubbles began to form.

"Increase speed," Gabriel said. "Thirty knots."

The ship began to move, the rattling dissipating as it sailed forward inside the bubbles. No, not bubbles. One bubble. Like a sleeve of steam and air. "Do you feel that?" Peter asked.

"What?" Gabriel didn't feel anything.

"We're moving at thirty knots, but we're not vibrating a tenth of what we would be normally. And we've stopped shaking."

They were sailing along through the water. The reading said thirty knots, but... "Can you gauge our actual speed?" Gabriel said.

"I can." Misty brought up the sonar on her own tablet. She saw the shadow of a whale in the distance and tapped it. "Blue whale, two miles away."

The shadow of the whale grew as the sonar beeped, and they suddenly passed it, the beeping dying.

The ship was nearly silent, cutting through the water in its bubble as the ocean slicked around them. "Guys," Misty said. "We're doing two hundred and fifty knots."

"Hoooooly mackerel," Gabriel said, suddenly unable to suppress a laugh. *Two hundred and fifty knots!* That was almost three hundred miles an hour.

Peter had a smile the size of Kansas as he hovered his hand over the throttle control. "Captain, we have a ship with no oxygen but a heck of an engine. You ready?"

"Yeah," Gabriel said. "Set course for Antarctica. Full speed."

Peter slid the accelerator on the tablet far to the right, and at five hundred knots, the *Obscure* shot through the water like a sunken jet.

21

THE ESCAPE DINGHY was a strange craft to spend a long time in. It was surrounded by Nemoglass windows, so normally if you were riding in it, at least you could look out at the sea or at the choppy surface of the water. But riding in the pocket where it was kept, using it essentially as a life-support chamber from which to control the ship, the only thing to see was the black inside of the *Obscure*'s hull. There wasn't even the usual feel of the waves, because the *Obscure* was flying along inside a pocket of air—to Gabriel the ride felt like a voyage in a coffin.

"Okay, guys." Peter hauled up his backpack. "What is the one thing you have both forgotten that I never forget?"

Misty put her elbow on the back of the driver's seat and glanced at Gabriel in the back. She shrugged. "What?"

Peter opened his pack. "Food. Seriously, you two must run on adrenaline or something."

Gabriel laughed as Peter hauled out everything he had grabbed from the coolers next to each of their stations. Peter handed Gabriel a seaweed-wrapped package of kimbap and a banana.

"Misty, I found you another banana, and I guess this is a veggie wrap." Peter fished out her veggie meal and handed it to her. It was also wrapped in dry seaweed.

"What did you bring?"

Peter looked in a bag on his lap. "I have some Jordan almonds and some chocolate-covered espresso beans."

"So, candy," Misty replied. "*You* run on candy."

"And to drink..." Peter hauled out a pair of water bottles. "Water. I didn't have any cola, except I did bring"—and here he handed Gabriel another bottle—"some of your weird kelp soda. We always have plenty of that. It will never run out." He muttered, "Never, ever."

Misty happily tore into the veggie wrap. "You're amazing, Peter."

"Yeah, just wait." Peter reached in and brought out one last item, brushing it off and sticking it to the dashboard of the dinghy. It was Misty's Troll doll.

As they watched the bubbles race by, Gabriel devoured the lunch Peter had packed—it was close to half past three in the morning, but he still thought of this as a *lunch*—and felt his energy rise again. The three of them chattered like monkeys, seeming to agree to put the present emergency aside without even saying it. They talked about the *Obscure*. They relived every moment they'd had on the ship, the fiery rescue of the sinking pleasure barge and the chase by an enormous sea creature that had put on the skin of an old English warship. And finally they rested.

After some silence, Gabriel said, "There is a possible problem."

"What now?" Peter harrumphed.

"Antarctica is very different from what it was a century ago. One thing the Nemos never pictured was global warming."

"You're worried the trench might be different?" Peter said.

"I'm worried the way the *Nautilus* went might not even be there. Antarctica is melting and shrinking. Dumping, what?"

Misty nodded. "Losing about two hundred forty billion tons of ice every year. It's *changing*."

"Okay," Peter said. "So, there's that. We follow our maps and hope for the best."

Finally, traveling at a depth of three hundred feet, the *Obscure* began to run out of air. Gabriel looked over at Peter's tablet as an alarm flashed. "What do we have?"

"Oxygen generators are nearly depleted."

"I mean, they'd have to be," Gabriel said. They had been traveling for thirteen hours in the cramped dinghy.

Misty showed him the sonar from the front seat. "Gabe, we're just a few miles off the entrance to the Weddell Sea."

Gabriel looked at the sonar. A shaded land mass—really an ice mass—indicated the vast sheet of thick ice over very—very—cold water.

"Good," Gabriel said. "Let's surface for air and then proceed under the shelf."

"Surfacing," Peter said, and the ship around them began to quake. The air bubble had dissipated to just a few bubbles here and there, and now sunlight turned the water green as they rose to the surface. When they emerged, they were looking at a landmass of ice that stretched across the horizon as the *Obscure* rested on a slick mirror of water dotted by icebergs.

For a moment, Gabriel stared at the glimmering blue-and-white landscape. "It makes you want to get out and run around." He was the only one who could dare say it because he was the only one who absolutely couldn't, not with just twenty-four hours to go. The bladders of air in the ship filled quickly, even running fresh air to the dinghy. They waited only the ten minutes it took to be sure they were pumping air again and then submerged.

Peter had to be careful now that they were closer to ice—the engines ran roughly ten times faster than expected, so he needed to keep the ship at what amounted to flank speed to maneuver, so perfectly did it slide through the water with the air cavity.

"Dive to one hundred feet," Gabriel said.

"Diving, aye," Peter echoed. They sailed down, sliding under the shelf, under rolling mountains of blue ice that made their ceiling.

"Gilbert Trench," Misty mused. "That has to be just a target, a general area. It's mostly ice itself—it's a big cavern, and by big, I mean Grand Canyon big. There would be liquid parts, but I have to think the *Nautilus* wouldn't have been able to get through the ice to it."

They traveled through the water for an hour until they reached the far edge of the shelf, where suddenly the ice of the ceiling and the floor came up to walls that ran for miles. Peter flipped on the outer lights, and they watched the great floodlights of the *Obscure* sweep across the ice walls as they tugged smoothly along. Peter looked back. "*Now* what?"

Gabriel didn't know. The wall they were looking at was practically endless, and they didn't have any hints beyond this. They all stared at the ice. "Options?"

Misty shook her head. "You're thinking it's in a cavern beyond the wall."

"Of course," Gabriel answered.

"There's volcanic activity all around underneath us. That plus global warming changes the ice, too. How much it would change in a hundred years, I have no idea."

"Was there an option in there?" Gabriel stared at the ice, a great *blank* waiting for him to come up with something.

"Sonar," Peter said. "Bounce sound off the ice walls. When we find something that has a different depth of ice it'll sound different."

"Okay," Gabriel said.

They swept along the ice wall for an hour and listened, keeping their sweep within the five miles of the wall that was closest to the Gilbert Trench, on the assumption that that was the most likely place the *Nautilus* had gone into an ice cavern.

Ping. Ping. The sound bounced back dully.

Then, a slight change. The ping came back faster and had tonally changed half an octave. "What's that?"

Peter brought the *Obscure* closer to the wall and they continued the ping.

"It's definitely something."

Misty brought up a NOAA map of the shelf and shook her head. "No, no, this"—she indicated the coordinates—"this is the entrance to a volcano. It probably stretches miles off to the right and down."

Gabriel realized he had been gripping the seat and now sat back.

They passed over the next two miles seeing little fluctuation. "Okay," he said finally.

"Look, it's...," Misty said.

"I know," Gabriel said. "If the ship went into a cavern, it might have been walled off a long time ago."

"Well ... it's metal, right?" Misty said.

"What?"

"The *Nautilus*, it's a metal ship. I mean it's this magic Nemo metallurgical geegaw stuff, but in the end it's a big hunk of metal, right?"

Gabriel said, "Yeah?"

"Uh, well, radio detects magnetic field fluctuations," she offered. "We could use the radio and the sonar to sweep and see if we detect any change in the sound of the static."

"Boy, is that a sentence," Peter said. "Are you suggesting ..."

"We make the *Obscure* into a metal detector."

Gabriel watched as a tiny, hot rivulet of hope crept across the glacier of hopelessness. "Try it."

Peter brought the radio online, saying, "We don't use this much. I think the last time was when we were playing chicken with the *Alaska*."

He turned up the volume so that static filled the tiny dinghy, pulsing in their ears. Misty turned on the sonar, and they heard the pings again, bouncing back close because they were less than a quarter mile from the ice.

They began at the edge of their search area, moving across the wall, the static reverberating, fluctuating here and there but essentially changeless.

They heard the sonar change when they slid past the underwater volcano and swept on.

And then, a mile and a half from the end, the static changed. The sonar altered slightly, only slightly, but the static ripped higher.

"Volcano?" Gabriel asked.

Misty looked on the maps. "Down underneath, but not right here."

"Gabriel," Peter said, "there's metal beyond that wall."

Gabriel wanted desperately to have them all be right and say *we've found it*, but he had been wrong before. "All right. Then let's figure out how to look at what's there."

22

22:14:09

ALONG DIM, RED-FILTERED corridors, Gabriel and Misty hurried through the *Obscure*. The refreshed air they'd brought in from the outside was sweet, but Gabriel knew it was flowing out again with every breath. They made it to the passenger compartment in forty-five seconds and donned their deep-sea suits. They would need them here, not for depth but because the water outside was deadly cold and the suits were built for that contingency.

They armed themselves with pincer sticks—clublike wands with rubber handles and heads that could spark with energy, for close-up use—and a flare or two each, clasping the gear to their belts.

Misty didn't jump around this time. "It already feels

like the moon," she murmured, the lights from her mask casting streaks of white in the compartment.

They moved in augmented steps toward the bridge. Its door was hanging open, and Gabriel was struck by its desolation, the sonar map still up on the screen, the rest of the bridge in shadow. They hurried down the ladder to the torpedo room.

"I guess I spoke too soon. We're going to need these after all." Misty knelt by a stack of pincer torpedoes.

Normally she would set the power of the missile through a series of menus at her station, but that wasn't feasible here. The torpedo tubes had been rejiggered to work the air bubble. And without the tubes, the menus on the bridge were useless. Luckily, they could arm them directly through a series of collars on the torpedoes themselves.

"You sure you can fire those by hand?" Peter asked in Gabriel's ear. "You could try to undo what we did to the torpedo tubes."

"We're going to need the supercavitation drive," Gabriel said. "And we won't have time to rebuild it."

Misty hefted one of the torpedoes. It was about seven feet long, roughly the width of a large coffee can, and capable of delivering arcs of energy powerful enough to cripple a small ship. "We can't just fire them out of our hands," she said. "Not even in the suits. But if we set it, it should drop as we swim away. It'll fire by itself."

"So all we have to do is aim." Gabriel nodded. "And hope it's enough."

Half an hour later, Gabriel and Misty floated in ice-cold water three hundred feet from the spot on the ice wall where their metal detector had lit up.

Gabriel listened to his own breathing through the apparatus at his mouth, and he could see condensation inside Misty's mask.

Like Misty, Gabriel held a torpedo in front of him in the water. It was taking everything he had not to drop it. Misty's torpedo was about three feet from his as she struggled to hold hers. The suits worked—he could barely feel the cold. But he found it tougher to do little movements and strained to get his elbows to bend enough in the thick material.

He just hoped they would deliver enough heat to punch a hole in the ice wall.

Gabriel waited with his torpedo while Misty cranked a series of raised bands around hers, sliding numbers on the band until the one she wanted rested against an arrow on the torpedo. "Maximum," she said. She looked up and handed the torpedo over. Gabriel let it roll across the one he was holding, then dropped his original one into Misty's outstretched arms. She made quick work of setting it as well.

Gabriel looked past Misty through five hundred yards of dark water to the *Obscure*, which floated with its lights dim except for the one flood lamp trained on a specific spot on the ice wall. That spot was the target.

"Okay," she said. "Peter, we're gonna fire."

"You're swimmin' around with missiles," Peter said. "Seems a waste not to."

Gabriel looked at the wall and held the torpedo to his side, and Misty was the perfect mirror image. "Aim."

"Aim," she said. "You think we're far enough back?"

That actually made him laugh. Every little thing was dangerous.

"I think so." He thumbed a rubbery button and felt a click through his heavy gloves. "Arm."

"Arm."

"I set a six-second delay," Misty said. "Swim fast when you drop it."

"Copy," he said. "On three?"

She nodded, and he saw her wince through her mask as she held out the torpedo in the water. They counted.

"... Three."

Each thumbed the last button.

"Fire."

The torpedo came alive in his hands and rumbled, and Gabriel swam backward, whipping his arms fast as the missile quickly dropped ten or eleven feet.

Suddenly the torpedo lurched like something coming alive, bobbing for a second before the engines in its aft section burst with blue flame and shot away. Its fellow left the water in front of Misty and the two missiles traveled together, at one point along the way trading places, long trails of gas bubbles hissing behind them.

A blinding flash lit up the wall of ice as the torpedoes hit. Arcs of blue energy crackled and crept along the wall as the ice exploded. Enormous bubbles of steam erupted, shaking the water all the way back to them.

The arcs of energy kept flowing for a full minute, as they were programmed to do, in theory able to sweep through a ship, turning its engines and radios to slag.

Then all went dark except for the floodlights from the *Obscure*. Gabriel didn't want to breathe as they swam the distance, whipping their legs until they reached the wall. But he could already see one thing that made his heart soar.

Before them lay a jagged hole in the ice wall, about three feet in diameter, and beyond that, the black darkness of a cavern.

"We opened a cave!" he shouted. Yes. *Yes.* They swam in. The lights on their masks lit up the rocky ice, and then they could see almost nothing as they entered a reservoir of water whose dimensions Gabriel could not determine.

Misty thumbed the flashlight on her shoulder, and it lit up the cavern more as she swept around. "I see hints of the wall over there." She pointed to her right. "Man, it's dark."

Gabriel swore he felt something bump along his right leg, but nothing was visible. He decided it was his mind playing tricks on him—probably just the belt on his left boot—and put his mind on the cave.

They floated a few yards when Misty stopped, looking up. "Do you see what I see?"

Gabriel followed her eyes, which were deep behind the condensation in her mask. "It's light." Above them he saw glowing brilliance, like you might see as you neared the surface of the ocean in daylight. Except that was impossible, because they were deep under a glacier.

"How could there be light above us?" Misty asked.

"It could be a crevasse that goes all the way to the top of the ice shelf," he offered. "Let's go."

Kicking their legs and swimming steadily but slowly, they rose, ten yards, then twenty. The light grew. They were approaching a surface, a pocket of air, and now he could see orbs of light, blurry through the water but distinct from one another. Multiple light sources. They were nearly there.

Wherever *there* was.

The water gave way as his head popped over it, his arms splaying out, treading as he looked up. Misty's head bobbed a few feet away.

It was a cave of glimmering ice, the water black in comparison. But what amazed Gabriel most was a metal lattice strung across the sparkling frozen wall, from which were hung at intervals amber blocks in the shape of familiar swirling shells, which glowed and lit up the cavern. Were they really in the right place?

"What in the world?" Misty looked along the wall. "Is this..." She spun in the water and looked at him, throwing back her diving mask, and then she fell silent.

Gabriel was about to say *what*, but something in her staring made him stop. Misty treaded water but seemed unable to speak, her eyes aimed past his shoulder. Slowly, Gabriel turned until the rest of the cavern filled his vision.

There before him, resting on the surface of the water, was the *Nautilus*.

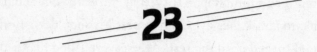

23

21:44:39

IT WAS IMPOSSIBLE to take it in all at once. Gabriel treaded water, backing up toward the icy ledge of the cavern, and gulped, unable to convince himself it was real.

The first things he saw were the scales, large black sheets of specially forged metal very like that on the hull of the *Obscure*. These sheets were big, some six feet long and twelve feet high.

And the scales went back and back along the hull. He knew without having to wonder how big the Nemoship *Nautilus* was—two hundred and ten feet long, about four times the size of the *Obscure*. It lay partly submerged in what Gabriel now saw was an enormous hangar. All along the walls, he could see rows of orbs of light giving a warm glow to the whole place.

"I . . . ," was all he could say.

Was it real? It was here, it had to be, but all the disappointment of the search spun through his brain, and he couldn't place two thoughts together. He bumped into the ice ledge behind him and turned to climb up onto the path that ran along the wall. Without him hearing, Misty had already climbed out and was offering him a hand. He glanced quickly at her and took her hand, climbing out, barely controlling his limbs, his attention still on the submarine.

Standing on the ice ledge, he now took it in—the ice cavern hundreds of feet long to accommodate the hidden ship. "I can't believe it!" He jumped in place, and even though he slipped a bit, he still wanted to jump again. He hugged Misty in a great bear hug as he called the *Obscure*. "Peter, we've *found* it."

"What?" Peter's voice came back in almost a croak, as if Peter could hardly believe it, either.

"Yes. The *Nautilus* is here, it's in a . . . a giant sort of ice garage. I mean, looking around, I think a crew went to work enlarging this thing." He scanned the ceiling, seeing traces of tooled carvings and endless cables of shell lights. "There are lights, hundreds of them."

Gabriel looked down. "Did that cave seem big enough . . ."

She read his mind. "For the dinghy? Yes."

"Peter," Gabriel said, "you got us this far. *Get up here.*"

Less than ten minutes later, the dinghy surfaced in the ice hangar, and Gabriel was still running back and forth on the ledge. His need to get inside the ship was killing him, but he wanted Peter to be a part of it.

Peter brought the dinghy to the ledge and climbed out with Misty's help. No sooner had she dragged him up by the arm than he turned and let out a whoop. Gabriel ran between them, and they locked arms.

They spent what must have been a minute hooting and jumping, hugging, saying again and again, *We found it. I can't believe we found it.*

Peter stared past Gabriel at the long ship—not as giant as Nerissa's *Nebula* but still a pretty big sub—and said, "It's amazing, it really does look like the model." Gabriel had shown them the *Nautilus* among a collection of models at Nemolab not long ago. "*Way* better than the prop."

"Look at the scales," Misty said.

"Yeah!" Gabriel ran along the ice ledge. They were alongside the middle of the ship, and he ran toward the front, seeing the hull curving until the nose came into view. "Look at the prow—it's true, it's a corkscrew prow."

"Just like a narwhal's horn," said Misty. That was why newspapers had first thought Captain Nemo's ship was a monster, because when it attacked ships, it punched holes in them. The professor who had investigated Captain

Nemo had thought that it was more likely not a monster but a giant narwhal, which was essentially a whale with a unicornlike horn on its head. Surfaced here, the *Nautilus* resembled a black narwhal at rest.

"Gabriel, do you have your—"

Gabriel gasped. "I can see the insignia on—the shoulder!" He ran along the walkway, coming around to see the forward starboard bow. There was the crest of the family, etched into the bow and lightened so that the *N* shimmered in the light.

"Misty." Peter cleared his throat. "*You* have your Geiger counter, right?"

She did, and Gabriel distractedly saw Misty pull out the device, which was about the size of a TV remote, and sweep it in the air. "Normal," she said. "Of course, we haven't been inside."

"Inside," Gabriel said aloud. He could barely get the word out. Inside, he had to get inside. He wanted to call his sister, though he couldn't do it from deep inside this cavern. But she had to know. *They had found it.* The words kept repeating in his head.

He looked far down toward the rear of the ship. The propeller, which he knew to be twenty feet in diameter, was not visible but lay below the water.

Nearer him, all the way forward on the part of the *Nautilus* that *was* visible above water, was the pilothouse, correctly trapezoid shaped. He was struck by the height of the real one. The little housing rose about five feet from the hull of the *Nautilus*, with long, frost-caked windows along it for the crew to see out if they were moving close to something else and needed to watch the hull. Behind the housing was a platform where the crew could gather atop the sub.

At the end of the ice ledge was a metal catwalk that extended to the platform and the little window house of the *Nautilus*. Gabriel gestured to Misty, who scurried after him as he stepped on the catwalk, trying its sturdiness a few times by stamping his foot on it while he kept his other foot on the ledge.

He was shaking. Literally shaking. "I—"

"Hey, man," Peter said. "It's a Nemoship. You belong on there."

Gabriel took a step and set his foot on the platform right next to the window structure.

He bent down and used his elbow to scuff some of the ice away but could see nothing inside. But as he went around the rear window of the pilothouse, he saw a recessed handle in the metal next to the glass. He put his hand on it and looked back at Misty and Peter. "You ready for this?"

Misty came and crouched next to him, then handed him the Geiger counter. "If you're going first, I want you to carry this."

Gabriel took the Geiger counter, whose little LED display still read NORMAL, and gripped the handle. He turned it and pulled, expecting the panel with the window to open up.

But it didn't—instead, as he stepped back, the platform he was standing on began to slope down, folding into stairs. He had just revealed a staircase that went down into the ship.

"This whole section can retract," Gabriel said aloud. Remembering what he knew from the models, even if they weren't wholly accurate, helped him regain his composure. Still, he heard a slight rattle in his voice, and his skin was tingling. "The pilot windows there, that whole structure, it can pull down into the hull so it's just a big gray cigar." He hadn't set foot on the stairs yet. Clearly—incredibly, after over a hundred years!—the ship still had power, allowing the stairs to form. He could make out dim light inside. He looked back at the crew. "Let's go."

"Heck yeah." Peter came in behind Misty.

They stepped down the stairs into a wide room—twenty-four feet wide, he knew—with several metal seats that protruded from the walls like an octopus's tentacles. A wide cylinder extended from the roof down to a hooded visor, and next to it a pipe that ended in a splayed-out shell design. "This is the bridge," Gabriel said. "Periscope and, uh, command megaphone." He reached out and gingerly touched the periscope tube, then looked up at the wall. A large map of the South Pacific lay under glass, with marks of grease pencil on the glass itself. He could see that several other maps had been retracted—you could slide them out and display wherever the *Nautilus* was.

Peter ran to one of the consoles. "Navs. It's funny, it looks almost like ours, just... wood, and there's more handles."

Gabriel laughed. Then he swept around in a circle. "Okay," he said. "You know what the question is, right?"

"Yeah." Misty sounded a little distracted herself as she looked around. "Where is everybody?"

They began to search the *Nautilus*—through the galley, which was spick-and-span and devoid of food. Through the bunks of the crew, which looked to Gabriel like the separated gills of a fish.

They came across a set of red curtains separating off a section of the ship, and Gabriel froze in place. "Oh, wow."

"What?" Peter asked, coming up behind him.

"Do you know what this is?" Gabriel's voice croaked. He held out a hand and found he was shaking. He pushed back the curtain.

He looked back at Misty and Peter, unable to speak as he stepped inside. He looked around, taking it in, extending his arms as though he could absorb it through his fingers. The room felt large, even though he knew he was on a sub. Wood panels curved to the ceiling behind delicate, Victorian furniture with cushions of red velvet. A solid gold globe sat on a great oak desk and turned of its own accord, still run by some eternal Nemotech battery, as though spun by a ghost. Beyond the desk was a pipe organ that gleamed with silver, its ivory keys dusty and tan with age.

It was the great salon of Captain Nemo.

"*Wow.*" It was all he could say. He put his hand on the globe, feeling the tiny carvings of continents slide under his fingers.

"What is this?" Misty asked.

"This is where he..." Gabriel shook his head. *Was himself? Was what we all think of?* "This is his sanctum."

Peter cleared his throat. "We gotta search."

Gabriel was still shaking. Yes. Right. "Right!"

"You can stay here."

"No." Gabriel took his hand away from the globe. "If I do, I'll never leave." To the laboratory next. The lead wall they'd read about was there, and beyond it, making no register on the Geiger counter, a wooden table that was only partly visible as they stood in the doorway.

And there was no one. Not a soul.

"A hundred and ten years," Gabriel said. "There would be..."

"If they were here," Misty said, "they would still be here." Meaning their *skeletons* would be, most likely.

Gabriel couldn't wrap his head around it. And then he saw his own wristwatch, and it all came flooding back: He was being a fool, he had a mission, and it wasn't to find the missing *Nautilus* crew or to gawk at this ship. No matter that it felt practically alive. They had a goal. An urgent one.

Gabriel held out the Geiger counter, and it gave no response as they stepped to the lead wall, which was about five feet tall. He looked around it to see more of the table.

There, on the table, lay a lead cask. It was bigger than he had expected, about three feet long and half as wide. On the sides and on the top were carved a symbol:

"Whatever you do," Misty said, "don't open it."

Gabriel ran his hand along the lead to the simple latch at the top. If the journal was correct, the silver cask would be inside this. "How do we know if the inner cask is still here?"

"I don't know, but the silver cask is likely to be

radioactive if the device was," she said. Then the eye on the top of the cask caught the light just so that it glimmered. Gabriel realized it was slightly raised and dared to slide it to the side. Below the eye was a thick layer of Nemoglass, a window.

He saw the glint of silver, and a circular seal in the top that looked like a machine gear. "It's there," Gabriel said.

"So—it's a yard-long box," Peter said. "A lead box."

"Yeah, it's gonna be heavy."

"I don't think you can fit that thing in the dinghy, not with us," Peter mused. "I don't know how we get this out of here."

Gabriel shrugged. "We'll float it," he said. "There's bound to be buoys on this sub."

A loud slamming sound cut through the air near the table, and Gabriel jumped, looking to the bulkhead. The wall curved up and was probably several feet thick, so whatever it was must have been large or have hit them hard. "Did you hear that?"

Wham. Something dull colliding with the hull outside.

Peter's eyes grew wide. "What if it's ice?" he asked. "What if the cavern is breaking up and chunks of ice are falling?"

"Hang tight." Gabriel and Misty began to jog through the ship, down the main corridor, to the bridge where the staircase still lay open. There were no chunks of ice on the stairs, but Gabriel had to agree that Peter's theory was sound. What if they'd triggered something in the engines of the ship, and that change, the first in a hundred years, had caused the cavern to fall apart?

But as they stuck their head out, no broken ice revealed itself.

They climbed out onto the platform, looking around. The strange lights still hung there, lighting up the enormous hangar, large enough to hold a lagoon that could house a two-hundred-foot submarine. But that wasn't his concern just yet. Gabriel stepped to the edge of the platform, looking into the black water, perfectly still against the metal hull.

Misty gasped from the other side of the platform, and he looked back.

Whump, another heavy sound of something slamming into the metal, and now something slipped from the water, showed itself, and disappeared. Gabriel felt his skin crawl.

It was the long-finned tail of what appeared to be a moray eel. He saw it again for a moment, silvery white and disappearing in the clear water, sliding along the hull of the ship. And then another came up, moving in the opposite direction. On and on it slid past them, and Gabriel watched as its mouth, full of razor-sharp teeth, flexed as it went.

"Is that a moray?" Gabriel asked.

Misty pursed her lips. "If so it's a long way from home. And it's silver-white like it belongs in a cave. So I don't know. Antarctic cousin?"

"So...a moray," Gabriel concluded. They were not friendly fish—the moray eel is a hungry and resilient snakelike fish that can extend its jaws, alienlike, and is eager to remove your thumb or your foot, whatever is convenient.

"That's got to be..."

"Twelve feet long," Misty replied. Gabriel was shocked to hear a tremble in her voice, because he had never heard her scared. "Oh," she said. He followed her eyes. There were more. Many more. He heard the water sputtering as they flipped through the surface and down.

"Where did they come from?" Gabriel watched a bunch of the eels swarming around the dinghy as well. Like they smelled dinner.

"They're silver. I think they're not even used to light. I think we let them in here," Misty said. "They probably followed us."

"I felt something bump my leg when we were treading water," Gabriel said. "Do you think..."

A *glurge* sound smacked in the air, and Gabriel looked over to see an eel come out of the water and slither along the hull and back.

"Oh, nope nope nope," Misty said.

"You said it. Peter?" Gabriel asked. "It's not going to matter whether we can fit the box on the dinghy."

"Why's that?" Peter came back. "What's going on?"

"Because we can't get to the dinghy." As Gabriel and Misty slowly spun on the platform, the water of the cavern teemed with what must have been hundreds of eels.

Gabriel looked at Misty. "You think maybe we can pilot the *Nautilus*?"

24

20:57:12

GABRIEL RAN HIS hand along the instrument panel in front of him, upsetting a coat of dust. The instruments were made of polished wood, the panels ringed with metal and padded with a dark gray leather. As Peter had said, it looked like earlier, less-digital versions of the controls they used every day. The soft amber glow of the instruments in the bridge meant one thing.

"This ship has power," Gabriel said. "At least enough to keep these lights on, *and* the lights on the walls in the hangar. Let's see what else we have."

"I can't believe they've got sonar." Misty slid into a chair in front of what appeared to be a sonar screen.

Peter found a wheel about the size of his palm with a diagram that indicated it twisted clockwise, increasing power as it went. "I think this is the throttle," he said. "I've seen a design like this on some old equipment at Nemolab."

"We don't have a diagram of the whole bridge?" Misty smirked.

"I'll get right on that after we start the ship. Wait." Gabriel's attention was caught by a small amber lamp with a switch, AUX and MAIN, right next to where Peter was sitting. "Wait. Main power." He put his finger on the switch. "You guys concur?"

"Oh, yeah," Peter said.

Misty was looking under the panel at her own feet and looked back up at him. "You're asking me?"

Peter flicked his hand. "You go take your post next to the megaphone; this is Navs."

Gabriel said, "Look, I like the idea of driving this ship. But I gotta be honest, it might be unstable after all this time. With that in mind, you can say no." *Please don't say no.*

Misty's eyes told him she wanted to drive the ship as much as he did. "Hey, it's this or the eels."

Gabriel nodded at Peter, who flipped the MAIN switch.

All around them, the ship began to thrum, vibrating softly through the walls and deck.

Misty gasped as she sat back up in her seat. "Sonar is online!" Gabriel looked over to the circular glass display in front of Misty—it showed the sweep of an arm and the shape of the cave they were in—essentially a cigar inside a much larger cigar. "There's not enough room to turn around in this cavern," she said. "Can you pilot it backward?"

"I don't know if I can pilot it at all." Peter found another switch marked AFT and hit it, and a new amber light glowed. He hit FORE, and Gabriel felt that, as the vibration intensified below their feet.

"Life support?" Gabriel scanned the ceiling.

Misty got up, looking along the other positions in the bridge. "Life, life, life support, got it," she said. "There's a gauge here with a needle, reads *normal*."

Gabriel shook his head. "If it's normal, where is everyone?" he asked softly. But finding the crew wasn't the mission right now. "Good ... Okay, what about depth control ..." He looked around and spotted it, a wooden handle on a half wheel on the wall marked off in hundreds of feet. "Misty, can you handle elevation while Peter handles direction? Prepare to dive."

She went over the strange nineteenth-century instrument and grabbed it. "Depth control, ready."

"Reversing engines." Peter flipped a switch and swiveled the throttle. "Let's see if we can move."

Gabriel felt the ship rumble and grabbed on to the captain's periscope pole as they began to slide backward. "Are we moving on the sonar?"

Wham. They lurched, the whole ship clanging to a stop and seeming to bounce. Gabriel nearly fell over. "What is it?"

A buzzer was sounding. Peter looked several feet over and saw a glowing light and ran to it. "CHOCKS. Chocks?" Chocks were something used to keep a vehicle from rolling around. He pointed at a metal plate on the wall of the bridge, showing an outline of the *Nautilus*. It was ringed with little lights, and one was glowing in a spot directly at the bottom of the hull.

"We're held in place."

"Probably chains," Misty said. "Something like that. If they knew they were going to be here a long time, they would not want the ship to start drifting."

"Options?" Gabriel asked.

"We could try to break them."

"I don't recommend that," Peter said. "We could tear the hull away. Look, it's probably just a hook, or a pin or something. But if those chains are holding the ship, we don't want to try to tear them off."

Misty sighed, crossing her arms. "So..."

"Yeah." Gabriel was looking at the diagram and picturing the mission at hand. "We gotta dive with some eels."

25

20:48:06

GABRIEL TAPPED THE button on his pincer stick, and it began to spark at the top, ready to zap anything it touched. He held it at a distance from himself and looked at Misty as they stood on the platform atop the *Nautilus*. The hangar was louder than it had been before, rumbling with the sound of *Nautilus*'s engines and the sickening slapping of eels as they swarmed, snaggletoothed mouths snapping.

"Do you think they can chew through the suits?"

Gabriel shrugged. "Remember the worms?"

Misty shuddered. They'd run into worms that blazed at one point, and they'd found out that the suits absolutely were not armor. "Okay. We slide down, we keep back-to-back when we can, and we sweep."

Gabriel nodded. "You ready?" The snapping mouth of

one of the eels seemed to say *it* was certainly ready. He looked down at the eels. "Guys, I'm not some porpoise or baby seal. I'm another creature entirely."

"Ready," Misty said. They nodded and slid along the hull.

For a split second, they were in the air, and then they plunged in the water, eels scattering in momentary confusion. "Drop, drop," Gabriel said, and they pointed their legs, side by side as they started sweeping the pincer sticks. They began to spin, sweeping the sticks behind them, the plates of the hull flying past. The eels had been startled by their appearance and only now started to come closer as they reached the bottom of the ship.

"Back-to-back," Misty said, and they went shoulder to shoulder. They left about a foot of space between them, and it was harder to swim now. But back-to-back meant they only had to guard their front. An eel swam close, and Gabriel swatted at it, the pincer stick arcing. It swam away and circled as more swam past.

They scuttled awkwardly sideways, using their legs and arms to move along the underside of the hull. The water burbled with the sounds of the creatures while their joint servos sang out. Gabriel looked up for a moment at the hull as they passed, wishing briefly that he had time to study it. There would be time later.

He felt something brush his boot and yanked his foot

up, sweeping down with the stick, an eel squirming back, snapping its jaws.

Misty turned on her forearm lamp and shone a light ahead of them as they swam sideways together and lit up the underside of the ship. Still dark. "Where is it?"

An eel came straight for Gabriel's mask, and he zapped it right in the side of its bulbous head. Arcs of energy crackled around it, and it spun away.

And then there it was. One moment they were looking at black water and eels, and then suddenly a great chain with links nearly half his height drifted into view.

They had to keep sweeping the sticks as they scuttled toward the chain and took in the attachment to the underside of the ship's hull. One link appeared to be permanently part of the ship, clearly ready to sweep up and into its own indentation. A golden pin as big as Gabriel's forearm connected that link to the rest of the chain as it went down out of sight.

A hole had been burrowed into the end of the pin, with a thin cable attached to it that snaked down into the darkness as well. Gabriel grabbed the cable and tried to yank the pin out. "It's stuck."

"Yah!" Misty swatted at an eel. "One of them took a chunk out of my fin."

Enormous pressure, the pressure of a whole ship pulling against the pin, made it impossible to just slide out. Gabriel looked around. "There's got to be something to make it easier. They would have had to do exactly what we're doing if they wanted to unhook." He tested the weight of the cable. "This feels loose but weighted."

"Haul the cable up," Misty said urgently, avoiding the eels. More of them were gathering, their teeth shining in the water. "Hurry."

He put his pincer stick under his arm and began to haul the cable with both hands. After a moment, out of the blackness below them, came a hammer with a thick, metal handle. "Okay, I got it, you have to hammer the pin out."

He reached for the hammer and then dropped it as an eel appeared, and he swept his pincer stick at the creature. Then he began to haul again. "Sorry. Got it."

"You get the pin," Misty said, "I'll guard."

Gabriel didn't wait. He gave her his pincer stick as she got right behind him, sweeping both the sticks.

The hammer was large, slightly bigger than a sledge, and he reared back his hand—swatting an eel in the process—and swung. The pin sang when he hit it and budged slightly.

"Hurry," Misty said again, zapping another eel. One of them got past her and tried to nibble on Gabriel's shoulder, and she zapped it next to his head. He could feel the turbulence in the water as they swarmed, and she began moving faster. He hit the pin again.

It moved again, and he felt something click out of place.

The pin was suddenly moving freely, sliding through a groove set in the chains. It was almost all the way through. He grabbed the pin on the other side, prepared to hit it on one side and guide it on the other, when he saw writing.

ALL HANDS——

—was carved into the pin.

"There's writing on it," Gabriel said.

"What? Would you hurry? Argh," Misty said. He could hear her zapping and the eels' excited burbling.

He hit the pin again and jerked his other hand back as it came free. The link attached to the ship snapped into its crevice in the hull. And Gabriel nearly dropped the pin as the chain dropped instantly into the water below. But he managed to hold on and, despite the danger, took a second to look at the writing. On the length of the metal rod, in deep letters, someone had engraved:

ALL HANDS TO THE TIGERS

What?

"Gabriel!" Misty shouted, and he heard a bursting crackle. He looked back as an eel lunged, grabbing one of her sticks and yanking it. Gabriel spun, slipping the pin under his belt and kicking with his fins to move next to her. The eel that had grabbed the pincer stick was bouncing away, shocked, but the stick spun off into the depths.

Misty was down to one stick now. "Fight through them; use your elbows and knees." Misty swept the stick as she and Gabriel went back-to-back again, bashing.

Gabriel was moving as fast as he could. His arms were starting to ache. Every moment, another snapping jaw came close.

"Peter, we're coming back," Gabriel said. *I hope.*

They swam, moving as fast as they could, Misty crackling at the eels. Gabriel elbowed one that came at his waist and kneed another. *Swim.* Any second now. They began to see the light of the surface.

They surfaced and scrambled, Misty handing Gabriel her pincer stick to swat at their pursuers while she hauled herself onto the handholds of the ship. Gabriel hustled up behind her.

The water popped endlessly with the sound of the eels. They got up to the platform and Gabriel looked back at the hangar.

"I never want to do that again," Misty said.

"You're telling me." Along the ice walls, the eternal bulbs glowed on. He pulled the pin out of his belt and scanned the inscription again. *All hands to the tigers.* What did that mean?

But now wasn't the time to find out. Not with Mom in danger half a world away.

~~

They gathered again at the bridge of the *Nautilus*, and Misty shouted, "Chocks away!" as they found their places again.

"Reverse, one-quarter power," Gabriel called.

"Aye." Peter slid a handle. The sub rumbled louder, and once more they felt the ship sliding back. Amazing. After all this time.

"Yes!" Misty looked at the sonar screen. "We're moving backward in the hangar."

"When we got in here," Gabriel remembered, "we swam through a tunnel. Was it wide enough for this ship?"

"Plenty," she answered. "I'm sure of that. It was probably how the *Nautilus* got in here in the first place."

"Plenty?" Peter shouted. "More like *barely*. But it'll fit."

"Dive, one hundred feet," Gabriel called. "Back through the tunnel."

The ship was moving smoothly, perfectly balanced.

"Dive, one hundred feet, aye." Misty yanked the handle down. Now the *Nautilus* shuddered as ancient caverns in the walls filled with liquid and they began to sink, something that Gabriel could feel in his bones. Misty read out from a gauge next to the handle filled with liquid, a needle sweeping along it. "Seventy-five...one hundred." Suddenly she whispered, "Whoa."

"What?"

"Check out the sonar screen." The line that swept around the sonar screen no longer showed the narrow lagoon they were in, for they had dropped into a much larger reservoir many hundreds of yards wide, a great circle at the end of the tunnel. "I can see the entrance to the tunnel onscreen, but Gabriel, we have *plenty* of room to turn down here."

"Good . . . Peter, one-eighty degrees left rudder."

"Aye." Peter looked around, finding a rudder control at the station next to him. He hopped out of his curved metal seat and grabbed a swiveling handle. "Left full rudder."

The ship was backing up at about five knots and now began to sweep its nose to the left as its aft section swept to the right. Gabriel could feel the weight of the ship, and his body drifted on the deck as they turned the ship around. At 230 feet long, it took several minutes, and Gabriel walked over to the sonar screen to watch it happen. He looked back at Misty and Peter and smiled. Finally, the *Nautilus* was pointed outward.

"Okay. Peter, straighten out and head for the tunnel. Misty, dive to two hundred feet."

"Dive, two hundred, aye." Misty ratcheted the control. "That should put us right at the mouth of the tunnel."

"Increasing speed," Peter called. "We need to be doing about forty knots."

"For what?"

"The *Nautilus* has a battering nose," Peter answered, "but I'm betting we need speed for it to work right."

The ship barely registered the increased speed as they began to move faster. The *Nautilus* slipped under the lip of the tunnel, and they were moving along the same tunnel Gabriel and Misty had swam through in darkness. Gabriel wished he had cameras and a view screen, because he would have liked to see the tunnel they'd swum in through.

Had the crew chosen it because it was a natural phenomenon that would accommodate the *Nautilus*?

"Sonar reads we're one hundred feet from the entrance," Misty said. "I mean, from that hole we blew in the entrance with the torpedoes."

"It's okay," Gabriel said. "This ship was made for punching." The narwhal horn at the front of the ship was ready for some ice, and they had already drilled a pilot hole for it.

"Collision, eight seconds," Peter said as the sonar beeped in alarm.

"Peter, full throttle. And hang on," Gabriel said, and Peter throttled the engine again. They sped up.

The *Nautilus* shook as the ice gave way. Gabriel could hear chunks breaking off and sliding around the hull.

At full speed, the Nemoship *Nautilus*, lost for over a hundred years, punched its way out of the ice and rejoined the inhabitants of the sea.

26

20:22:20

PETER USED HIS remote to bring the dinghy and the *Obscure* back to the surface, and after thirteen minutes, the three vessels—the *Nautilus*, the *Obscure*, and the dinghy—lay in the sparkling sun, side by side. He extended the *Obscure*'s walkway, and it clicked into place on the scaled hull of the original ship.

Gabriel walked out to the middle of the walkway between the two craft. Short, choppy waves lapped at the metal and up over his boots. Two miles away, the water turned to ice, and the horizon was white as far as the eye could see. The wind whipped bitterly cold against his skin. "So what do we do with the *Nautilus*?" Peter took off his glasses and polished them with his shirt. The wind was so cold that Peter's teeth were chattering, and Gabriel realized his were, too. They needed to get inside.

That was enough to bring Gabriel back to earth. "We're gonna have to submerge the *Nautilus* and rest it against the ice shelf. It'll keep until we come back for it. I hope." The odds of someone stumbling across it all the way down here seemed long. It was the best he could do. He couldn't wait to get it safely back to a safe space, though. He shrugged toward the *Nautilus*. "This is . . . I can't say how great this is, but it's not really the *Nautilus* we're supposed to be finding. We have the cargo. We have to hand it over."

"Is the Dakkar's Eye radioactive?" Peter asked.

Misty shrugged. "It's shielded."

Peter put his glasses back on and pushed them up his nose. "So . . . and I don't mean to be crazy, but assuming it is, are you really going to hand a radioactive box over to a bunch of terrorists?"

Gabriel sighed. He still didn't know the answer to that. "We have twenty hours until the deadline. Let's call Nerissa."

They gathered on the bridge of the *Obscure*, and the air inside was still thin, the fresh air from outside only starting to replace the foul air that had been circulating. "Open a secure channel."

Misty tapped at the Nemotech intercom. "Go."

"*Nebula*? This is *Obscure*, come in."

Nothing for a moment. Then they heard the sound settle into a dull echo. "*Obscure?*" Nerissa sounded urgent. "Where are you?"

Gabriel didn't want to answer that, but he rolled his shoulders to release the tension and just said it. "Uh . . . well, we're about ten miles off the Gilbert Trench."

Nerissa paused. "The Gilbert Subglacial Trench? What the— Why are you at the South Pole?"

"Technically we're still about a thousand miles from the South Pole."

"Gabriel!" Nerissa hissed. "Technically you're about seven thousand miles from *me*, and you know where I am?"

"Don't you want to know—"

Nerissa cut him off. "Look, it's coming up time. I'm going to rendezvous with Dad near Midway Island."

Midway Island lay in middle of the North Pacific, once the landing point for planes headed from California to Hawaii. A helpful dotted line appeared between their current location and Midway. Nerissa had been off a bit, and the reality was worse: She was nearly *nine* thousand miles away.

"What are you planning?" Gabriel asked.

"I'm going to catch up to them, and I'm going to board them," Nerissa said. "We're going to extract Mom."

"Oh, no no no," Gabriel said. That could be incredibly dangerous. He had hated this idea from the moment she'd started talking about it. The Maelstrom would have one chip to play: Mom. They could hide her, they could hurt her, they could even kill her. And all it would take to trigger any of that would be tipping them off. "Don't do that. It's too dangerous. Look. I can bargain with them."

"With what?"

"With the Dakkar's Eye," he said. "We have it in a lead box. Or we will as soon as we drag it over the catwalk."

Nerissa started to say something, then stopped. He heard a thump—an elbow? A fist? Her head?—on a table. Then almost a whisper: "Are you telling me you found the *Nautilus?*"

"We didn't just find it," he said. "We have the *Nautilus* surfaced at the Weddell Ice Shelf. It's floating thirty yards off our port bow."

"I...I want to..." Nerissa sounded like she couldn't keep her thoughts straight, and Gabriel knew the feeling. "Send me a pict— No." Then she was silent for a long time. Long enough that for a moment, Gabriel thought maybe they'd lost her signal.

Misty pursed her lips as she folded her arms. "Never thought I'd hear *her* at a loss for words."

"Don't send any pictures," Nerissa said. "Antarctica, it was in *Antarctica?*"

"Yes."

"I can't believe you actually found it." Nerissa was whispering, almost to herself. "What about the crew?"

"It's strange," Gabriel said. "There's no trace. I don't

know. That's gonna take some figuring out." *All hands to the tigers*. Whatever that meant.

"Okay," Nerissa said. "This changes things. I don't want to hand over the Eye, but if we have it, we need it in our back pocket. But…" And she swore as she realized again the distance. "You're *days* away. Maybe we can bargain."

"We don't need to." Gabriel made a quick explanation of the supercavitation drive.

Nerissa listened and then summarized: "You broke your ship to make it go faster. That's pretty…amazing." *Amazing* didn't sound like something she approved of, but whatever.

"I didn't break it," Gabriel said. "It's just…we're doing what we have to do to help *her*." Gabriel looked down, his cheeks flushing. The *Obscure* was his home, as much as Nemolab. But if he had to make a choice between one of the most important *things* to him in the world and his mom, his mom would win any day. "The *Obscure* will pull through."

Nerissa didn't answer that. The statement hung there, daring him to doubt it himself.

"Anyway, it was only possible because we don't have, like, hundreds of extra people," Gabriel said. They could never have done anything like the supercavitation change-up with the *Nebula*. There would be nowhere to put the crew when the sub stopped pumping breathable air through the compartments.

"No, it's pretty brilliant," Nerissa said. Still more polite than usual. Still stunned about the *Nautilus*, he knew. Gabriel could sense her fighting not to turn the subject back to the lost ship. "Can you move the Eye? Really move it? I don't want you blowing yourself up."

"We can move it." Gabriel looked at Misty, who nodded. They would want to wear lead clothes. Lead everything. "We'll put it in the personnel carrier room."

"How quickly can you get here?" Nerissa asked. Peter looked at Misty, who came back with . . .

"Sixteen hours if nothing gets in our way."

"Holy mother of mackerels," Nerissa whispered. "All right. We gotta keep our eye on the ball. Submerge the *Nautilus* somewhere and mark it. Then rendezvous fifty miles south-southwest of their position. I'll send you the coordinates."

"Okay," Gabriel said. "Then what?"

"Then we talk to the Maelstrom, and one way or another, we are getting our mother back."

27

17:25:37

FOR THE SECOND time, the crew crammed themselves into the escape dinghy and submerged. "Boy," Peter said as they dropped to two hundred feet, the rush of air bubbles beginning to drizzle along the side of the hull. He looked around at the closed windows that showed nothing but interior hull metal. "I'll never think of the *Obscure* as small again."

"You thought of it as small?" Misty asked.

"Well, there's the *Nebula*," Peter pointed out. "That thing could swallow us. We ready?"

"Ready. Hit it, Peter," Gabriel said from the jump seat. "Let's go find them."

There was a jolt as the air flow outside increased and steam on the hull hissed, the bubble forming, and then they were thrown back against their seats as the *Obscure* shot forward. Gabriel felt his insides settle, and then he leaned forward. "Now. We have seventeen hours to work with. I recommend we take shifts, and each grab five hours of sleep. Misty, you can go first."

Suddenly the ship lurched, and Peter yelled, "Whoa, whoa, whoa."

They were still moving but slowing, the ship juddering in the water. Gabriel could feel the vibrations hitching. He had never felt the *Obscure* move so unevenly. He leaned on the driver's seat. "What is it?"

Peter showed him the pad. "Something's wrong with the engine."

"Do you know what it is?" Misty asked.

Peter stared for a moment at the diagram. The engine room was lit up orange. "No."

Gabriel breathed. "Okay, surface. Let's check it out."

A few minutes later, as the *Obscure* floated on the surface and fresh air circulated through the ship once again, the three of them crammed into the engine room below the bridge.

Gabriel and Misty were shining handheld lamps as Peter crawled around underneath the great black housing of the engine. Gabriel hunched down to keep from hitting his head on a large pipe and talked to Peter's legs, which were sticking out from under the engine. "Well?"

Peter's voice was muffled. "*Yee-ah-aa-ahh.*"

Peter scuttled out and, lying on his back, grabbed a rag from nearby and wiped thick streams of oily black from his hands. His face was smudged. "I was afraid of that."

"Give it to us straight, Doc," Misty said.

Peter sat up, gesturing with the rag. "The propeller's not meant to spin in the air."

"Meaning what?" Gabriel didn't follow.

"Well, we made a sub into an airplane, and the bubble is the sky, right?"

They both nodded.

"And our propeller usually is pushing against the weight of the ocean. So all this time we've been running it, we've been moving about ten times faster, and the propeller has been moving easily twice, three times as fast as usual. Now what causes the propeller to turn is, like any engine, pistons and rods that are driven by the energy of the—"

"Fast-forward," Gabriel said.

"Thank you," Misty said.

"It's burning out the engine," Peter said. "What *could* have happened is that lots of stuff just broke, but instead a safety kicked in and the *Obscure* stopped."

"Why now?" They didn't have time for this.

"It's probably been on the way to happening the whole trip. Now, because there's a crack in the connecting rod. If it broke completely, the engine would never run again."

Gabriel nodded. "Well, we gotta keep using the

supercavitation process, so...I assume you can fix it?" They barely had time for that. "Because if we go back to the standard engine, we don't..."

Peter shrugged. "Gabe, are you listening? You're assuming that I can get it to run at all."

Gabriel dropped to a crouch, shining the light. There was a pool of black grease smoking under the engine. "Work the problem. Options?"

Peter pointed. "So, okay...we have to keep the supercavitation, so whatever we do now has to prep it to continue moving way faster. The thing that's showing wear is the rod, so let's assume that if we fix that, we're fine."

"Fine," Gabriel said. It didn't sound fine, but... "And the solution would be?" He rolled his hand.

"Can we fix the crack with Nemoglass?" Misty asked.

"What?" Peter asked.

"Nemoglass, it's built to withstand tons of pressure. You said there's a cracked rod, that's like a metal rod, right?"

Peter nodded, holding his hands apart. "About three feet long."

"We can't melt Nemoglass here," Gabriel said, "even if we had an extra window to pull apart and melt down and slather onto the rod."

"Forget melting it," Misty said. "You have a cracked metal rod, what do you do with a cracked bone? You splint it. If we had a sliver of Nemoglass, we could use regular adhesive to splint the rod. Is there room for that?"

Peter thought. "Yeah. But where are you going to get this Nemoglass splint?"

"Again," Gabriel said, "all our windows are in use. But for the rest of the ship..." In his mind, he was running through the *Obscure*, looking at everything. He needed a smallish bit of Nemoglass. Once he had seen a coffee cup made of Nemoglass, presented to an ambassador as a gift. But generally they didn't just throw Nemoglass around. He moved his mind to the back of the ship. "There are two dive suits—they have Nemoglass masks," he said.

"You can't use those," Misty said. "We might need them."

"I agree."

"Wait," Misty said. "The Katanas have retractable Nemoglass windshields. The windshield is in three sections. They're about two feet tall. Would that work?"

"You get it here," Peter said, "and we'll see if we can glue it on."

It took twenty-five minutes for Misty to return with a piece of the windshield of one of the Katanas, and by that time Peter had set to work taking care of a bunch of other things just in case. He had Gabriel bring much heavier oil up from storage to mix in, and he also ran a diagnostic on the energy shield. Fortunately, it looked okay. Misty was dripping wet as she burst back into the engine room with a slightly curved section of Nemoglass, about a foot wide and two feet long.

Gabriel grabbed a gun for applying an adhesive normally put to work to fix exterior holes and used it to attach the piece to the rod. "Don't get that on your hands." Gabriel handed Peter the gun.

"You're telling me." Peter held the end away from him and the Nemoglass in his other hand and dropped back, disappearing under the engine. "I still have airplane glue on my hands from the bridge model."

For a few moments, he worked, and Gabriel and Misty waited. Misty folded her arms. "What do you think?"

I think we're killing the ship, Gabriel wanted to say. They were making things up as they went along, tearing apart pieces that he and his family had spent years bringing to life. The *Obscure* was a life to him, as carefully balanced and calibrated as a dolphin. But his mother was out there, and his *Obscure* was going to bear the brunt of the fight to save her.

"Anything to get her back," he said.

Peter slid out. "Guys," he said, "it ain't pretty, but I'll bet it can fly."

Back to the dinghy they ran, quickly, because every moment was time lost and they were still down at the bottom of the world.

They shut the metal wall behind them and climbed in, and Gabriel said, "Peter, set a course for Midway Island."

Peter monitored the ship as the systems kicked on. "Engines. We're moving."

Indeed they were. "Yes." Gabriel clapped Peter on the shoulder.

"Air stream. Energy shield. There's the steam. And we're in the bubble."

They fell back in their seats as the ship accelerated.

"Supercavitation process is online," Peter said. "Now . . . I think we were gonna get some sleep."

"You want to go first?" Misty asked. "You've been working."

"I've been lying on a floor. You go."

"Don't have to ask me twice." She put her tablet into a rubber grip on the dash and settled back. Peter and Gabriel fell silent. Then Peter said to him, "You can sleep, too. It's better if just one of us is awake, and I can wake you up in a few hours." Peter was offering him an extra hour.

"Oh, I don't think I can sleep," Gabriel said. No way. They had found the *Nautilus*, and more importantly the Dakkar's Eye. His brain was on fire. Besides, he was sitting in a cramped jump seat. He might rest his eyes, though. He closed them.

Seven hours later, he awoke because Peter was reaching back and shaking his shoulder. *Unbelievable. The body just takes over if you're tired enough.* "How are we doing?"

"Steady as she goes," Peter said.

Misty yawned and shifted in her seat, and her eyes opened. "I can't believe I'm still with you people."

"You want to sleep more? Gabriel can take the ship," Peter said.

"No, I'm awake," Misty said. She held out her hand and took the tablet, then looked at Gabriel. "Nine hours to go, Gabe. You want to play a word game?"

He would have said, *At a time like this?* except that he was tired of his every waking thought being one of fear for his mom. "Sure," he said, adjusting in the cramped jump seat. "What kind?"

Misty folded her arms and tilted her head. "Uhh … Sea Creature Alphabet."

"Sea Creature *Alphabet?*"

Peter kept his eyes closed but said, "As in name a creature that starts with *A*, *B*, *C* …"

"Oh," Gabriel said. "Okay."

"*A* …"

"Anemone," Gabriel said.

"Barracuda," Misty countered.

"Chambered *Nautilus*," Gabriel said.

"Nah, I don't think that counts," Misty said. "We need a straight *C*."

"Uh, coelacanth," Gabriel said.

"What's a coelacanth?" Peter muttered.

"It's a fish with arms," Misty said. "Aren't you supposed to be sleeping?"

"You're making it so easy," Peter said.

"We'll whisper," Gabriel said. "Dugong. It's like a manatee."

"I know what a dugong is," Misty scoffed.

They played through the alphabet twice and moved on to oceans and seas. For the first time in days, Gabriel felt really rested.

~~~

Eight and a half hours later, Peter was sleeping and Gabriel poked his shoulder, awakening him as the recognizable glowing shape indicating the *Nebula* appeared on the sonar screen on Peter's tablet. "Peter, time to slow the ship down, we're coming to sixty miles off Midway."

Peter sat up and looked at the sonar. "Where's the *Nebula*?"

Misty pointed to the larger of two shapes on the sonar image. "Right here—and I have no idea what this little ship is."

The intercom crackled. "Whoa, space people," Nerissa said. "Welcome back to the North Pacific."

"What have you done to the *Obscure*?" came another voice on the intercom. It was Dad. "I swear you shot onto my screen like a comet."

"We made some modifications." Gabriel turned to Peter. "That little ship is the *Eclipse*; it's a personal sub of my dad's."

"You shouldn't go closer to Midway," Dad said. "They'll be watching for me to come alone."

So Dad still hoped to show up by himself and hand over his fake device. "Can we rendezvous on the surface?" Gabriel asked. "Just to talk it all through."

They agreed. "Surface," Gabriel said. As Peter brought them upward, Gabriel folded his arms in defiance. "If he still thinks he can hand over a fake, I'd like to see it."

28

1:24:58

"LET'S SEE WHAT you found," Nerissa said. The passenger compartment of the *Obscure*, big enough to hold the refugees from a sinking pleasure craft, still felt cramped to Gabriel as he, Misty, Peter, Nerissa, and Dad gathered around a table in the middle of the room. Dad had come from the tiny *Eclipse*—which looked very much like a quarter-sized *Obscure* and lay just off the starboard bow of the *Nebula*.

The air was flowing, because they had surfaced and oxygen had started to flow again. They had spent a few minutes cutting the oxygen tubes away from the torpedo tubes—ending the supercavitation drive for now—and re-attaching them to the air systems. In a moment, they would have breathable air again underwater. Even so, the ship smelled stale.

"Of course, but..." Gabriel gave Nerissa and Dad a hug, and they both seemed raveled and harried. When he pulled away, they greeted Misty and Peter. Dad was wearing his lab coat and hadn't shaved. Deep circles ringed his eyes. Nerissa looked crisp, and she had her *Nebula* headset hanging around her neck so she could talk to her own crew. They turned to the table.

Before them on the table rested two boxes: the lead box the *Obscure* had brought back from the *Nautilus* and the result of Dad's work of the last three days. Dad's own project—Gabriel thought of it as the Replica Eye—took the form of a large *Nautilus* shell crafted from Nemoglass.

"I didn't know what the Eye was supposed to look like," Dad said. "So I figured why not be a little poetic."

"What is it?" Misty asked, bending down to look at it. It throbbed from within with a bright pink light.

"It's a...lamp," Dad said simply. "But it does provide power. If you attach electrodes to it, you can probably run this ship for a while. And Nemoglass always looks the same, so there's nothing per se to indicate that it's not old." He shrugged. "We have to give them something."

"I don't know about that," Nerissa said.

Gabriel wanted to play out the fake scenario a little more. "How do you think the Maelstrom is planning to test it?"

"Assuming they will," Peter said.

"They will," Nerissa said. "I would."

"I'm assuming electrodes and they try to power something, like a machine."

Nerissa said, "I dunno, Dad." She turned to the lead box and grimaced. "And this is the thing itself. Do we know what it really is?"

"The best I can imagine," Gabriel said, "it *was* a power supply, and it ruptured, causing the accident that the diary tells about. But we're not reading any excess radiation now. Obviously, this lead housing was repaired before Captain Nemo and the crew abandoned ship."

"If that's what they did." Nerissa shrugged. "The way you describe it, it's as though they just hid the ship. Why they didn't come back...?" She shook her head. "There's just no way of knowing."

"Shielded or not," Misty said, "I'm not even crazy about the idea of moving this anymore. The lead box is tough, but we don't know how fragile the insides are."

"If we're going to hand it over, we'll have to move it," Gabriel said. They had met on the *Obscure* because no one wanted to move the Eye, but if they had to, they had to. He winced inwardly because he envisioned the box bumping into something just right and rupturing, and, who knows, maybe reducing the ship they were on to molten slag, a pocket of steam erupting around them. He looked from sister to father. "What do you want to do?"

Nerissa looked at her watch. "Soon we're gonna have to talk to the Maelstrom. And we plan our attack while we're doing that."

"We can't *attack*," Gabriel hissed. He had been listening to her talk about a rescue mission since the beginning, but he was tired of playing along. It wasn't realistic. "If we do that they'll be stung, and that'll be *it*. And I don't even want to think about what they'd do to Mom. Just because everything with you has to be an attack, doesn't make it smart."

Nerissa stood, if it was possible, even straighter. "Why don't you tell me a little more about what's smart, Gabriel? You've got a leaking bomb in your hold and a crippled ship to show for it."

"*Stop*." Dad clapped his hands on the table. "Just stop. If we start snapping at one another, we're done. And I'm not risking your mother because you're both exhausted." He looked at all four of them. "And you're all exhausted. I can see it. Nerissa, you've been hunting for days."

"I have also analyzed the images of the *Gemini*, and I think—"

"If you don't mind," Dad interjected. "For *days*. Gabriel has been to the bottom of the world. Oh, and *you* two"—here he indicated Misty and Peter—"you two are amazing for putting up with all of this, but I can tell you've barely slept yourselves. All of you have done *amazing work*. But now we have three options, and we have to think clearly. From now on there will be no more fighting."

"So let's decide—"

"*I'll* decide," Dad said. For a moment, his eyes watered, and he wiped them. "Whatever we do, it has to be on me."

They all stared at one another, and Dad said, "Okay?"

Nerissa and Gabriel nodded. "Yes. Okay."

Dad sat down, the Eye on his right and the fake on his left. "When I set out to make a fake, it was a desperate measure. I didn't think in a million years that we'd have the real thing. It was desperate because, let's be honest, if we assume they're smart, they will be able to spot the fake. So giving them the fake is the riskiest move in the short term." He gestured to the box. "But giving them the real thing— something that could possibly power a whole pirate navy, or do who knows what to a city...Gabriel, you have to admit that that's even riskier, long term."

Gabriel and Nerissa eyed each other.

Dad went on, "The least risky move is the rescue."

"And..." Gabriel gulped. "If that fails?"

"Then if we have any chance at all, we have to hand over the real thing."

Gabriel let it sink in. This was the way it was done on every ship. You argue your side. And then the leader chooses a course. And you commit.

"So," Dad said.

"So," Gabriel answered. "We're going for a rescue. Who's going to do it?"

"I have a strike team I can call up," Nerissa said.

"I don't think so." Dad steepled his hands. "When I look at these two crews, only one of them makes it their regular business to go around rescuing people. It's your plan—but it needs to be Gabriel and his team."

Nerissa breathed. "Are you sure?"

Dad looked up at her and nodded. Nerissa kissed the top of his head and then turned to Gabriel and hugged him again. Gabriel felt certain she was going to whisper something. *Don't screw this up*, maybe. But she didn't.

Nerissa let him go. "Done, then." She touched her headset and called, "*Nebula*, anything on the Bubo?" Nerissa's ship deployed numerous long-range flying drones she had named *Bubo* after the mechanical owl in a movie she had loved when she and Gabriel were together back at Nemolab. She pulled off the headset and laid it on the table.

A voice came back, "Yes. Infrared is picking up the twin sub about ninety miles north of our position."

"Thank you, Nemo out," she said. "They're coming."

"How are you gonna sneak up on the *Gemini*?" Peter asked. "Sonar will pick you up. They're gonna be looking for the *Eclipse* alone."

"We used whales to sneak up on the *Alaska*," Misty offered. "But we caught a migrating herd."

"Well, that's pretty cool. Who came up with that?" Nerissa scanned the crew.

"That was all her," Gabriel said.

Nerissa tapped her lip. "Do you think they would be okay with the trade coming from you on the *Nebula*?" she asked Dad.

He opened his hands. *Who knows?* "They never specified the ship."

"They know we wouldn't risk torpedoing them with Mom onboard," Nerissa said. "So it's not shocking that I would pick you up and escort you in the *Nebula*."

"Right," Gabriel said.

"So the *Nebula* doesn't have to sneak; she just rides up, like they're expecting."

Gabriel understood. "We're underneath."

"What?" Peter asked.

"He's got it," Nerissa said.

"We move into position below the *Nebula* so that they see one sonar blip and not two. And then when we're still far enough away . . . we dive . . ."

"Below the cold line," Misty said. "Below where sonar will catch us."

"And we try the rescue then," Gabriel said.

"You don't try," Dad said. "If you're doing a rescue, you have to succeed. All this talk about what happens next is wishful thinking."

"Sonar only reads about thirty miles. But when they're fifty miles away, we should be able to radio them," Nerissa said. "I want to do that first."

"Why?" Dad said.

"I want to make sure that Mom is still okay."

"And if she's not?"

Nerissa scowled. "If she's not, if they can't prove she's okay—this whole mission changes."

Within the hour, with the ships still surfaced, they gathered on the bridge, and Nerissa asked Misty to tune to the frequency that the Maelstrom had broadcast on when contacting them to deliver their ransom demand.

"This is Nemoship *Nebula* calling Maelstrom *Gemini*," Nerissa said.

"*Nebula*?" Gabriel mumbled.

"They don't know where any of us are," Nerissa whispered. "And we only want them to know about the *Nebula*."

"Nerissa Nemo." A male voice came on. It was slightly reedy, casual. It sounded like a trustworthy voice. "Your father is getting close to his deadline time."

"We will be escorting him, and I can assure you that you will not be fired upon. But I want assurance that Dr. Nemo is still alive and healthy." Nerissa continued, folding her arms and looking down. "Can you provide that?"

"She is healthy."

"Put her on. I want to talk to her."

There was a pause. "No. Do you have the Dakkar's Eye?"

Nerissa shook her head. "I need proof. I need to know that she's alive, or we can't make any trade."

Now the Maelstrom captain started to say something and then cut off. After a moment he said, "Hold for transmission."

"Say again?" Nerissa snapped.

"I'm sending you an image," came the response from the *Gemini*.

Nerissa tapped off the intercom and spoke into her headset. "*Nebula*, this is the captain. Whatever you get on the multimedia feed, I want you to forward it instantly to us at the *Obscure*." Then she nodded and snapped her fingers at the view screen, and Misty brought up a blank box that began to fill in.

The Maelstrom was sending them video. Black and white. Clearly a security camera. There was a subtitle below it that said STBD—DET. But no sound.

On the screen, Mom was a seated on a cot, her legs crossed as she leaned on her elbows. There was a tablet near her on the wall, blankets, and even some books and papers.

Gabriel felt his heart tighten as he saw his mom. She was right there. She looked…unhurt. But his blood boiled at the idea that someone would take her away from her loved ones and keep her in a small room just to get something they wanted. He had been haunted by images of her for the last four days, but now those fears began to curdle into something else, an anxiety mixed with rage that made him shake. Nerissa was talking, and he had to consciously tune her in.

"There's no proof that's a live image," Nerissa said. "*Gemini?*"

"As you can see, she is unhurt." The captain of the Maelstrom ship *Gemini* sounded tired. Like he was putting up with about as much as he could, and soon he would lay down the law.

"Who do you think you're playing with?" Nerissa said. "That image could be from anytime in the last hundred hours. How do I know this is live? How do I *know?*"

The Maelstrom captain sighed. They heard him turn away and mumble something. Shortly after, Mom looked up at the camera, as though a sudden sound had interrupted her. She stood up.

"You see?" the captain said.

"No," Nerissa said. "If I were you, I would have anticipated that. That's nothing."

"Do you have the Dakkar's Eye?" the captain asked. "You have very little to bargain with if you don't."

Nerissa answered with another demand. "Ask Dr. Nemo..." Nerissa looked around. "Ask..."

Gabriel whispered, "Anything random. Ask her the first letter of the trench near Nemobase."

"Captain, I need proof. I want you to ask Mom—ask the prisoner the first letter of the trench near home."

Another sigh. A long pause. Mom was pacing on the

camera, looking up and shouting. And then she stopped to listen. And then she spoke at the same time she held up an international hand signal.

D.

Nerissa closed her eyes and put out her arm, and Gabriel hugged her. "She's alive," Nerissa whispered.

"Are you satisfied?"

Nerissa cleared her throat. "Yes. Yes. Now I am."

"Do you have..."

"You don't want it," Nerissa said. "We have the Dakkar's Eye, but it is very volatile. Look, fellas, it's hazardous. There's a good chance it will blow up if we hand it to you."

"Why don't you let us worry about that?"

"You're not listening. If we dock the *Nebula* next to the *Gemini* and try to move it, it might explode."

"Our instructions are clear. We are going to meet you in one hour. And you will deliver the item." The line went dead.

Nerissa turned to Dad and the crew. "Is the *Eclipse* on autopilot?"

"Yes," Dad said. "If I'm not back in two hours, it'll dive deep and wait for instructions."

"Okay. Let's get going. Dad, you're with me on the *Nebula.*"

Gabriel nodded to Misty and Peter. "As soon as they're off, prepare to dive, mark the *Nebula*'s position and bearing, and set a course right under them—close. Less than a hundred feet."

Peter nodded. He looked a little unsure. "That's close."

"Fair winds, everyone," Nerissa said. "Gabriel. Bring her back."

Once they'd disappeared up the ladder and out, Peter took his station. Gabriel was walking to his chair, and Misty tapped his shoulder. She turned her tablet toward him. She was pointing to the video of the *Gemini*, the one sent as part of the ransom message. Nerissa had sent a version covered in notations. "I think I know how to get in."

29

00:16:45

THEY TRAVELED FOR nearly an hour below the long shadow of the *Nebula*.

"Nerissa?" Gabriel said into the intercom. "We're going deep and silent."

"Go," Nerissa said.

Gabriel nodded to Peter, and the ship tilted at an angle. In silence they dove to five hundred feet. "Below sonar depth, Captain," Peter said.

"Level off and head for the position of the *Gemini*." On the sonar, a position marker—not live, but a good estimate of where the twin sub was likely to be—moved slowly.

When they were within half a mile of the spot, Gabriel said, "Okay, stay down here until we reach their position, then head straight up underneath them."

They started to rise as sharply as they'd dived, and soon the twin sub was visible on the cameras as a distant shape. "How deep are we?"

Peter said, "One hundred and fifty feet."

"Good. That means Mom will be able to get out with a rebreather. Hold again when you're fifty feet below them and match their bearing. As soon as we're gone, dive again and head back to the *Nebula*."

Gabriel looked at the countdown. "Nerissa? You have..."

"I have to call them in fifteen minutes," Nerissa said. "And that will trigger the exchange to start. So that's how much time you have."

"As soon as they move your mom, she's gonna have a whole party escorting her," Misty observed. "So we absolutely have to get to her before."

"Yeah." Gabriel breathed. He turned to Misty. "Let's go."

As they ran down the corridor to the lockers, Gabriel asked, "We're sure Mom is on the right-side sub?"

"The caption read *stbd—det*." She sounded these letters out. "That's gotta stand for Starboard detention." Misty grabbed a hard case and filled it with the items they had ticked off en route. Smoke canisters. Pincer rifles. And a canister of liquid nitrogen.

The ship shook for a second. Gabriel looked up. "What was that?" he spoke into his mic.

"I don't know, I'll look into it. It sounds like the engine.

We're holding it together with chewing gum, you know," Peter said. "Go, you need to go."

Hold together, Gabriel thought, looking around. *Hold together*.

"Dive and head for the *Nebula*," Gabriel said again. "Soon as we're clear." Gabriel opened the dive room and started flooding it as soon as Misty was inside. They took pincer rifles from the locker.

Misty shuddered as she held the pincer. "Gabriel, we haven't talked about what we're going to do with these." He saw what she meant. They'd never used them on people before, even kidnappers.

"We keep them on low power," Gabriel said. "And only use them if we have to."

He pulled his mask over his head as the water filled the room, gave Misty the thumbs-up, and opened the dive iris.

Warm Pacific water surrounded Gabriel's body, and he was thankful that he could travel in a lightweight diving suit. He stretched his limbs, respecting once again the flexibility when he didn't have to be in a thick arctic suit.

He and Misty dropped below the ship and untethered their Katanas. The engines shuddered to life, and they hopped on, aiming for the vast metal latticework that ran between the twin subs of the *Gemini*. Soon the corridors of the *Gemini*'s connector bridge were zooming up in Gabriel's view.

"Look out for security cameras on that bridge," Nerissa's voice spoke in his earpiece. "It's probably swarming with them."

A large conduit of steel was closing in, and Misty and Gabriel both dove hundreds of feet, coming around under it. The conduit was about ten feet wide and ran all the way between the two subs.

They floated there under the metal for a few seconds looking for their planned way in, then Misty pointed farther along the underside. There were multiple small craft very like their own, fastened to a docking station on the corridor's hull. From the distance they were at, this looked like a mess of dangling equipment, which struck Gabriel as unwise because it increased drag and caused noise in the water. It should make them easier to see on sonar. Then again, the *Gemini* had snuck up on the Institute, so they obviously were handling it pretty well.

As they got closer, Gabriel saw that the equipment was a lot like their own—personal water propulsion devices, Katana-like craft, and a plethora of oxygen tanks secured to the bottom. Misty started looking around once they were under the equipment. "If they fasten their personal craft here, that means that somewhere very near here there has to be a way in."

She turned over, swimming on her back underneath the corridor of metal as Gabriel followed. Finally, she found a handhold and an iris-shaped entrance. "This has to be a Maelstrom dive room." Misty turned the handle, and the iris opened, and Gabriel followed her inside.

Sure enough, they were in a flooded compartment attached to the corridor. The compartment was about eight feet square, with several large glass portholes looking out into the corridor itself.

A pair of sailors in Maelstrom uniforms came walking from down the corridor on the other side of the glass. *If we could get one mission where we're not avoiding crew members.* He swam out of the way of the porthole as Misty looked around for the controls. Finally, she found the flood/drain controls, and shortly the water receded. They dropped their rebreathers and let them dangle at their chests.

Misty dropped a hard plastic case at Gabriel's feet, and he opened it. There was an extra rebreather for Mom, which he stuck in a pouch on his belt. Next, he picked up one of the two pincer rifles and handed the other one to Misty.

Gabriel felt his chest tighten. This wasn't like the *Alaska.* If they failed there, the worst that would have happened was they didn't get a journal. If they failed here, they could lose his mother. Part of him wished his dad had put less faith in him. But no. If Dad believed in him, didn't he owe it to him to try to meet that?

"Fifteen minutes are up," Misty said.

Gabriel slid the door open as Nerissa spoke in their earpieces, calling to the kidnappers. "*Nebula* to *Gemini*—are you there?"

The inside of the *Gemini* was mostly steel, silvery and polished. They were trailing water all over the floor, and Gabriel wondered if they should look for some way to towel off. The water could be anyone coming out of a dive room, but it would still leave a trail. He wished he had some way to mop it up as they had on the *Alaska*, but no. *Keep moving.*

Misty's eyes grew wide, and Gabriel spun around. A sailor was coming toward them, just emerging from around the corner. Misty leveled her pincer rifle and fired.

An arc of energy curled through the air and caught the guy on the shoulder, sending reverberations all over his body. He fell instantly.

"I'm sorry!" Misty whispered. "I just didn't want him to call out, or, you know, blow a whistle."

"It's okay," Gabriel said. "It's the way we have to play it." He ran over to the crew member and crouched, touching his neck. For a moment, he panicked—it was his call to use the rifles and maybe he was wrong about low power, and then what? They were murderers now?

But no. He felt a pulse. Alive but stunned. Gabriel let out his breath. They dragged the guy into the dive room, shut him in, and hurried along the corridor. At the end, an iris opened, and they were aboard the starboard twin.

"How long do we have until that guy wakes up?" Misty asked.

"Minutes," Gabriel said. "And as soon as he wakes up,

he's gonna let everyone know, so we do this now or we don't do it at all."

"*Gemini*, we're ready to transfer the Dakkar's Eye," Nerissa said in their ears. "Tell us where to meet you."

"But we haven't found her yet," Gabriel whispered to Misty.

"We'll surface," the Maelstrom captain responded to Nerissa. "And we'll bring the prisoner to the platform of the starboard bow. Dr. David Nemo will deliver the Dakkar's Eye across the gangplank. When we have assured ourselves that it is there, we will then send Dr. Yasmeen Nemo over."

Gabriel felt the ship rising. Misty felt it, too. "They're surfacing," she said.

At the end of the corridor was an elevator, and they hustled to it and ducked out of the way as a pair of Maelstrom sailors exited and moved back down the way they'd come.

"There's so many," Gabriel said. He knew there would be, of course. It was a ship full of crew—but in that moment he was painfully aware that with every step, they were one corner from getting caught. And that would mean doom for Mom.

Inside the elevator was a schematic of the ship. Gabriel tapped it. "Level seven."

He let the doors close, and he and Misty waited as the elevator car moved.

"Smoke ready," Gabriel said, and each of them pulled their smoke canisters, looping a finger through the pin. The elevator door opened with a ding.

One second to sweep the corridor with their eyes. What they saw was a long line of doors on the right and a long line of windows—probably imitation Nemoglass—on the left. But only one door had armed guards in front of it.

In unison, they pulled the pins on their smoke canisters and rolled them toward the guards as billowing smoke began to fill the air. Before the guards could do more than crouch into position with weapons at the ready, Gabriel and Misty opened fire with their energy rifles. Arcs of energy twisted through the air and smacked into the guards. Gabriel winced again. *We can't get comfortable with these things. Just one bad heart on one of these guys and we're killers*, he thought.

The two men staggered and went down. Gabriel hesitated. He should let them lay there, but pretty soon this whole place would be underwater. He gestured to Misty, and they dragged the guards to Mom's cell door.

Testing the door and finding it locked, he shouted, "Nitrogen."

Misty dropped and began to spray the door latch. Liquid nitrogen cools to −346 Fahrenheit, and at that temperature, metal turns to cottage cheese. After a moment, the latch was covered over in a slick, dense layer of ice.

Gabriel backed up and kicked the door. As it flew open, Misty turned and sprayed the window right behind them.

Gabriel bashed through the cell door. There she was, in that metal room, rising instantly from the little bed. Her mouth was open in shock. Gabriel stepped forward, reaching for her. "Mom, let's go."

"What?" Mom's mouth hung open in a shocked *O*, but a moment later she waved him toward her with a relieved cry, pulling him into a crushing hug. "How? How on earth?"

"How?" he said, blinking tears back. "How could we not, Mom?" He sniffed and pulled away. "Now, seriously. We gotta move."

"Dr. Nemo? Here." Misty stepped into the cell and grabbed Mom's rebreather out of the pouch on Gabriel's belt. "We brought you a rebreather. You'll need it."

"Misty?" Mom shook her head. "I can't believe he convinced you to do this."

"It didn't take convincing," she said.

Mom took the device and slipped it on.

They moved back into the smoky hall. Misty and Gabriel dragged the guards back into the cell and shut the door. It might let water in through the busted lock, but they'd be okay.

With the three of them alone in the hall, Misty raised the rifle and pointed it at the windows. "Be ready for water." Gabriel grabbed Mom and dragged her a few yards down.

"What are you doing?" Mom asked as Misty aimed her pincer rifle at the sprayed nitrogen on the window.

The glass shattered instantly. Water gushed through the portal in a hard-sideways geyser, and the corridor began to flood instantly. Water slammed against the door and sloshed back. Gabriel kept his hands up, warding off the geyser coming in from the window.

"We need to go out the window," Misty said. "Just wait for it to finish flooding."

They were forced toward the ceiling as the geyser disappeared under the rising water. Only their heads stuck above the surface. And then their noses, and they put on the rebreathers.

The corridor was a vessel of water, a long, full metal box, very like a swimming pool with one way out: the window they had just busted.

Gabriel nodded at Misty and she went first, swimming toward the portal. It was just big enough for her to swim through, and after Mom shimmied out, Gabriel was only barely able to get his own shoulders through, scratching one of them on a shard of plexiglass.

Now they hung in the water outside the starboard twin, and Gabriel pointed toward the unflooded corridor they'd come in. They swam down, watching as security guards ran to and fro, visible through portholes in the corridor. No one thought to look outside to see them.

They reached the Katanas, and Gabriel hopped on his after unfastening it. Mom got on behind him, putting her arms around him. They dropped as he turned on the engine, and then Misty whipped up behind him, and they flew away.

They headed for the *Nebula*, still in danger. But Gabriel had his mom behind him now. Nothing mattered more than that.

"We have Mom," Gabriel radioed as they sliced through the water. Gabriel could see the *Nebula* growing closer as they neared it.

"Copy. Copy!" Nerissa shouted with obvious joy. "Come on in. Uh... Gabriel, are you in touch with *Obscure*? Peter hasn't checked in."

"He was supposed to go to the *Nebula*... *Obscure*? Peter?"

After a moment Peter came on. "I'm here."

"Where are you?"

"I'm still on the *Obscure*." Peter's voice was dull and distant. "It's bad."

30

OUT OF TIME

MISTY, GABRIEL, AND his mom met the *Nebula* on the surface. The ship was moving fast, but Nerissa brought it down to about ten knots, just slow enough that Misty and Gabriel could bring the Katanas alongside. The *Gemini* would be on them at any moment.

Crewmen gathered on the platform atop the *Nebula* and lowered a ladder, which clicked into place on the hull of the ship. Gabriel worked to keep the Katana under control as waves whipped against it and water splashed in his face. "Grab on," he called. His mom didn't wait. She let go of him and scrambled for the ladder, and soon she was being helped up over the top by the crewmen. Mom disappeared into the *Nebula*, safe for the moment.

A moment later, Misty scrambled up, her Katana

turning end over end and disappearing in the waves. She held on to the ladder and looked back at Gabriel. "Come on!"

But Gabriel didn't come on. He saw awareness flash across Misty's face before he said it. "I have to go back for Peter."

Nerissa's voice came through. "I'm not even gonna try to talk you out of that. Just hurry."

Gabriel let go of the *Nebula* and dove, calling ahead to the *Obscure*. The rebreather made his voice sound muffled, but it was better than trying to talk—and think—while bouncing across the top of the water. "Peter, what's your status?" If it had been Misty there alone, it would be easy. She could send the *Obscure* to the depths to be repaired later, and she'd dive out.

But Peter didn't dive.

"It's bad," came Peter's voice in his earpiece. "It's what we were afraid of. Uh, the engine is breaking down."

"Breaking down?" Gabriel throttled the Katana, diving a little deeper, cutting through the waves like a missile. The sonar panel at the head of the Katana told him the *Obscure* was about a mile away.

"I have about a quarter flank speed. The engine is about to stall," Peter said. "It's not something we can fix with some glue and a windshield."

Gabriel tried to take that in. "Okay, head for the surface. I'm coming to meet you."

An alarm Klaxon erupted on the bridge of the *Obscure*, audible over Gabriel's headset.

"What is it?" Gabriel shouted.

"The *Gemini*," Peter said. "They're within a mile of us."

"That was really uncalled for, Captain Nemo," came the voice of the Maelstrom captain on the *Obscure*'s bridge speakers. The voice was audible in Gabriel's ear.

"Peter, patch me through." Fine. He would talk to the Maelstrom captain while he headed for Peter and the *Obscure*. *What's one more thing?* He touched a button and flipped the channel they were on. "Who's this?"

"You know who this is," came the voice of the Maelstrom captain.

Gabriel groaned. "I've been thinking about it," he said, "and you know something? Your values are completely out of whack."

"But you're not faster than us," the Maelstrom captain said. "Think how little you've accomplished."

"I'm thinking about it."

"You manage to bring your mother back to your side and you've won yourselves, what, a few minutes?"

On the screen in front of him, the *Gemini* had entered the circle and was racing toward the *Obscure* from several miles away. Gabriel flipped back to Peter. "Are you surfacing?"

"Ugh," Peter responded. "Elevation is damaged. I don't know . . . I don't know. Uh, maybe it's just the software. I'm gonna try and bring it back up."

Good. That calm in his voice is him working the problem.
Work the problem.

The sonar told Gabriel he was within a quarter mile of the *Obscure*. In a moment he would . . .

. . . see it. The black ship with its swirls of mother-of-pearl emerged into view as it moved slowly from his left to his right up ahead.

A message from the other channel. He flipped back.

"Your choice is to turn around and surrender the Eye to us," the Maelstrom captain said, "or we will seize it."

"I don't think that's gonna work," Gabriel said. He was coming up fast on the underside of the *Obscure* and dove down, dropping under the dive room. He grabbed the carabiner line from the body of the Katana and hooked it as he swept under and slipped off and the Katana whipped away from him to trail behind. He slapped the iris and waited for the lock to work. It seemed to sputter, and for a moment, he wasn't sure if it would even open, but then it snapped back, and Gabriel swam up into the dive room.

Waiting for the dive room to empty was agony; he opened the door when the water was at his shins, then ran sloshing into the personnel room toward the bridge. He flipped back. "I'm aboard, Peter."

"Welcome aboard."

The lights along the corridor were shimmering in and out. They were losing power. He unlocked the door to the bridge, his eye catching a plaque next to the door, OBSCURE, put there when they had launched from Nemobase. For the first time he felt it in his bones, and it ached. They were losing more than power.

Gabriel burst through the door and ran to Peter, slamming him in a hug before turning to take in the bridge. Under flickering lights, he saw alarm messages all over the view screen. Power was down to 15 percent. Engine barely online. Oxygen production was dead.

What. Have. I. Done.

But it was worth it. His mom was safe. And they—

"Still no elevation," Peter said. "I don't know what you want to do..."

"We're gonna get out of this," Gabriel said. As much to himself as Peter. *Think. Work the problem.* The engines were the main problem. He snapped his fingers. "What if we used the dinghy and tow cables?"

Peter was still trying to reboot the elevators. "Dinghy doesn't have tow cables."

"No, but we can ride it out in front and then cable it from the *Obscure*." He shrugged. "And then..."

"Tow the *Obscure*?" Peter said. "Sure, but the Maelstrom..."

An alarm rang out.

"Torpedo in the water!" Peter cried.

"Really?" Gabriel flipped the channel on his headset

and shouted at the *Gemini*, "You're going to blow up your prize?"

"Fifteen seconds to impact," Peter said urgently.

"Countermeasures," Gabriel shouted.

"Countermeasures, no, offline," Peter said.

"Evasive, Peter, careful."

"Salvage is a skill we're pretty proud of," the Maelstrom captain said. "We think when you're on the bottom there will be plenty of time to collect."

"No," Gabriel shouted. "Detonate, detonate, call it back, Captain. I promise you, you don't want to damage the Eye."

"Do you really think we're going to listen to you now?"

Peter's voice cut through the air. "Two sec—"

Then a sound he had never heard before—a distant snapping and groaning in the ship as the whole vessel rocked. Gabriel grabbed on to the side of Peter's station.

Peter sounded out what Gabriel was afraid of. "Hit, hit, Gabriel, we've been hit. And I think it dinged the Eye, because I've got a lot of heat coming from the passenger compartment."

"Flooding," came an automatic voice from the speakers. "Flooding."

"Uh … and the back of the ship is filling with water."

Gabriel ground his teeth, thinking. "Peter, where is the—" He looked up at the sonar screen. The *Gemini* was sweeping around and away from the *Obscure*, and in a moment, they would come in again for another hit. The alarms continued blaring.

It can't be, it can't be. In his mind was a chessboard, and his finger was inching toward the king. He had taken the pieces he needed—his mother was safe—but it was time to admit it. In his mind, the king was falling, about to clatter on the board.

Oh, I'm so sorry. His family had made this ship. Everything they knew had gone into it. He had helped design every rivet and swirl.

And it was time to go.

"We need to head for the escape dinghy."

Pause. Then Peter cursed and looked up.

"What?"

"The escape dinghy was hit," Peter said.

The *Obscure* was shaking now, and a rumble passed through the ship. The lights went out.

Then came back on in dim red. Gabriel's mind reeled. "That's . . . that's okay. But you and me, we gotta get off the ship."

Peter's eyes grew wide as he glanced at the bulkheads. His body seemed small in the red light. "Oh, Gabe," Peter answered hoarsely. "I don't know."

"Hey," Gabriel said. "We work the problem." The ship shook under him. "Now we can't use the dive room."

"You think I'm *diving?*"

"I *know* you are, but we have flooding, so we can't go through the passenger compartment, so we can't get to the dive room." He looked up and pointed at circular shield at the top of the bridge. The same one he, Peter, and Misty used every day. It was an iris decorated with the letter *N* and encircled in metal handhold bars, with a ladder leading up to it. "We're going through there."

"Through the ceiling?"

"Have you ever used a rebreather?" Gabriel let go and ran to the panel by the door.

"Don't you mess with me," Peter said. Then he looked at the sonar screen. "*Gemini* is coming about." Gabriel handed him a rebreather when he looked up.

"Put it around your neck and—what's our elevation?"

Peter took it and slipped it over his shoulders. "One hundred and sixty feet."

Gabriel shook his head. "Too deep to go to the surface."

"What do you mean? It's not crush depth," Peter said.

"Yeah," Gabriel said, "but have you ever done compression stops?"

Peter started shaking.

At about nine hundred feet, the sea pressure could kill a person, but at 160, that wasn't a real concern. The problem was that a diver needed to come to the surface slowly—no faster than thirty feet per minute. Otherwise gases in the body would cause bubbles and injure or kill you. Just one of those things about diving.

"Okay, okay, okay." Gabriel pinched the top of his nose. "Kill the alarm, please."

Peter hit a button and the alarm died. Now they were shaking in the sea, the bridge rumbling under their feet.

"*Nebula?*" Gabriel shouted into the ceiling as he flipped to their channel. "Depth a hundred and sixty feet, you need to pick us up."

"Copy," Nerissa said. "We'll put ourselves right off your starboard bow."

"Good," Gabriel said. He took a breath and turned to Peter. "Okay, listen. We're gonna need to flood the bridge and go outside, and then we don't go any higher—we just swim, uh, west. And then the *Nebula* will come get us."

"Flood the . . . Gabe, I can't." Peter's voice was strained.

Gabriel touched a lever, and the controller section of Peter's station popped out. He walked over to the ladder and scrambled up a couple of rungs. He showed Peter the remote. "Come up. I've gotta open the door."

"You've got to be kidding."

"They're gonna fire on us any second, now we gotta climb this ladder and gotta grab on to the bars on the ceiling."

Peter looked up. "I know, I just . . . it's water."

Gabriel held out his free hand. "Peter. I've got you."

Peter scanned the whole bridge, still next to his station. And then he nodded to himself, fast. He ran to the ladder and grabbed Gabriel's hand as Gabriel pulled him up. They climbed, and Gabriel grabbed on to the bars, swinging around to the side of the ladder. "Come on, grab on."

Peter scrambled up the ladder, holding on to the bars and hanging with his tiptoes on the rung.

"Steady?" Gabriel said.

"I'm goin' nowhere, man," Peter said.

Gabriel clicked the remote, and the door at the back of the bridge shot open. Water came roaring in as Gabriel put his rebreather in his mouth and Peter did the same.

A new alarm rang out, and Peter looked down at his station, his voice muffled by the rebreather. "Torpedo in the water!"

"Hang on," Gabriel shouted.

"Time to impact...," Peter answered, watching his station as the water roared over it. "Sixty seconds."

The water was rising fast, and they hung there, waiting for the room to fill. "We need it over our heads," Gabriel said. "Or the pressure will hurt us. We need to flood this room."

"Mm-hmm," Peter said. The water came to their chests.

Gabriel held his hand just below the iris. Water went over his head. When he felt it pass his hand, he pressed.

The iris snapped open, and Gabriel pointed and Peter swam, actually swam, kicking his legs as he moved through the iris. Gabriel waited until he was through.

He took another look at the bridge as the lights on the stations glowed in the water. *I'm so sorry.* Then he kicked and swam out into the ocean.

"We're out," Gabriel said. He swept his arm to Peter, who hung in the water like a mannequin. Gabriel grabbed him by the shoulder and said, "We did the hard part. Let's go."

"Hurry," came Nerissa's voice. "Impact to *Obscure* imminent."

They swam, ten yards, twenty. Thirty. Gabriel gripped Peter's shoulder and spun them both in the water as the rocket slammed into the body of the *Obscure*, just under the nose, burying itself deep in the ship. A heavy *whump* shuddered through the water. Long strips of mother-of-pearl scattered from the impact site, shining as they spun in all directions.

Gabriel saw red spouts of flame burst through the portholes as the *Obscure* seemed to sway and stagger in the water. And then it began to sink, sawing back and forth like a dead leaf.

Both of them gasped, unable to say a word. Then Gabriel felt a shift in the water and a deep hum, and as he turned, a whalelike shape appeared from the shadows, the enormous ship *Nebula*. Gabriel let it pass before them until they saw the glowing lights of the lockout trunk. He tugged Peter's shoulder. "Let's go."

The lockout trunk door flew up, and Peter let go, swimming like a ragged animal. Inside, floating in the water, was Misty. She reached out her arms and grabbed him.

The three surfaced inside the lockout trunk, and Gabriel and Misty hugged Peter. "You did it," Gabriel said.

Peter threw off the rebreather as he climbed up onto the walkway around the pool. "I can't believe it."

"I can." Gabriel and Misty got up on the walkway, too, and the three of them fell together in a hug. "I can believe it."

"Okay, well," Peter said, his voice shaking, "Let's not do that again."

Nerissa's voice came over the intercom. "Gabriel, are you aboard?"

"Yes," Gabriel shouted.

"We're engaging them," Nerissa said. "I saw that hit the *Obscure* took. You should get up here."

"Okay," Gabriel said. "We're on the way."

They made it up to the bridge of the *Nebula* as the *Nebula* was firing on the *Gemini*.

"Negative, negative," the weapons officer said. "*Gemini* deployed countermeasures."

"Captain," the helmsman said. "*Gemini* is still pursuing the *Obscure*."

"Of course they are," Gabriel said. "They intend to pluck the Dakkar's Eye off the ocean floor as soon as it hits bottom." *Like grave robbers*, he thought.

"Go after them," Nerissa said.

On the screen, long-distance cameras showed the *Gemini* was closing on the *Obscure* even as it sank, full of holes and burning.

How could I sacrifice my ship? But he had saved his mother. And Peter. And that *had* to be worth it.

Right?

"Onscreen," Nerissa said. Long-range cameras showed an infrared image of the two subs, the *Obscure* diving and blazing hot. "That must be the Dakkar's Eye glowing like that. But *look*, they're trying to *catch* it."

"How can they?" Gabriel asked.

"Well, *you'd* try to haul it," Peter said. "But *I* assume they're gonna just follow it to the bottom and salvage the prize from there."

Gabriel watched the *Gemini* pursue his sinking submarine and said, "I guess that makes sen—"

And then an orange ball filled the screen and snarled through the twin ship *Gemini* as the Nemoship *Obscure* exploded.

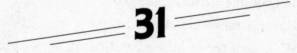

31

THEY HUDDLED IN the inner sanctum of the *Nebula* as they traveled back to the school. Gabriel sat across from Peter, who was shivering with a blanket around him.

Nerissa poked her head in. "Dad is with Mom. You want to come see them?"

Gabriel looked up. "How is she?"

"She's good. She's... wound up and exhausted. I've got her in my stateroom. It's... nice."

He nodded. "I'll come see them."

When she was gone, Gabriel looked back at Peter while he and Misty sat in silence.

"Peter, I'm sorry," Gabriel said. "I never..." He searched for words and looked at Misty, who didn't try to give him any.

"Don't," Peter said. "I know what you're saying, but

don't. Listen. The supercavitation drive was my idea. And it did damage to the ship. But it's what we had to do."

"But I was pushing," Gabriel said.

"And yeah, you push." Peter laughed. "But I'm not *drafted*, Gabe. I could have said no. For real. I could have said no. Or, by the way, I could have not been so brilliant, because again, the supercavitation drive was *my idea*."

"The ship broke because I couldn't give up on the idea of finding the Eye," Gabriel said. "Or really, finding the *Nautilus*. But when we started this, I promised you wouldn't have to swim."

"Gabe?" Peter cleared his throat. "I'm afraid of water. That's just a thing that's true. But when I had to get out of there, you helped me, and I did. It's done. I trust you." He looked at Misty. "We trust you. And you have to trust us. Not just to do what the mission calls for, but to know what we're doing."

Gabriel looked down. "I'm just sorry."

"Okay. I hear you." Peter got up and clapped Gabriel on the shoulder. "Apology accepted. I'm sorry the *Obscure* didn't make it." They hugged, and Gabriel had never felt so much gratitude in his life.

"Now go see your mom," Peter said.

Gabriel walked down that hall, and the *Obscure* was gone. It was strange because every thought was like that, *I am walking down the hall, and the* Obscure *is gone. I am knocking on a door, and the* Obscure *is gone.* He tried to push it out of his head. *I am pushing the* Obscure *being gone out of my head, and the* Obscure *is gone.*

When he knocked and Nerissa opened the door, he saw his mother and remembered the reason for everything. *The* Obscure *is gone, but Mom is safe.*

Mom and Dad were together on a love seat, shoulder to shoulder, and they both rose instantly. Again he put himself in a three-person hug and felt their warmth. Mom pushed back after a moment, looking at him, running her hand over his face. "You're all right? Everyone is all right?"

"Everyone is perfect," Gabriel said. "It was scary. It was really..." He touched his own eye, blinking away a tear. "They did so well. And I'm so glad you're here."

Dad hugged him again and spoke into his hair. "Thank you."

"It's okay," Gabriel said.

"You held it together."

"I don't feel that way." Gabriel shook his head. "I've been...one step behind all along. I made so many mistakes. Dad, I lost...I lost the ship."

"No," Dad said. "You may have lost a ship, but you held it together. You want to know the truth? You held it together better than I did. I fell backward into analyzing. You and Nerissa did that and more."

"Don't..." Gabriel didn't know how to process what his dad was saying. It was too generous and made him feel weird. He looked at Nerissa, who stood nearby. "It was hard on everybody. We all did it together."

Gabriel's stomach rumbled, and it snapped him to the reality that they had been running practically on fumes. "Are you guys hungry? Mom, you'd have to be."

"Oh, absolutely," Mom said.

"You don't even have to ask," Nerissa said. "I'll have something brought in. But first..." She spoke into her headset. "Navs?"

"Captain?"

"Set a course."

"For the Institute?" Mom asked.

"For Antarctica," Nerissa said. "To pick up the *Nautilus*."

EPILOGUE

TIME ENOUGH

THE TRIP THAT the *Obscure* had managed in a day took the *Nebula* five. Gabriel spent most of that time with his parents, just taking in their presence.

"Have you heard from the Maelstrom?" Gabriel asked as he looked out of the Nemoglass wall in the aft stairwell, which gave a panoramic view of the Pacific as they rocketed southward.

Dad shook his head. "No. We picked up chatter from them, but there's no sign that the *Gemini* made it."

"Why…" Gabriel stopped and looked out. A cloud of colorful yellow tangs and clown fish burst across the window and disappeared in the distance. "Why didn't you tell me about the Maelstrom?"

Dad ran his hand through his hair. "We really wanted to spare you all that. But obviously that was a mistake."

"What was a mistake?"

"We wanted to spare you from knowing that there were people who wanted to keep us from doing what we do. There's nothing worse than knowing that someone hates you. But I guess when we started the experiment—reaching out to the surface world—we owed you the information."

They turned and started up the stairwell with the ocean swirling in colors behind them. Dad stopped and turned, looking at Gabriel. "Do you have any idea what it's like to have you guys in our lives, you and Nerissa and Peter and Misty?"

Gabriel furrowed his brow. "We do our best."

"You succeed."

~~~

Gabriel's mom and dad came with Nerissa, Gabriel, Peter, and Misty down to where the *Nautilus* was submerged, just fifty feet below the surface and barely ten miles from the ice caves where they had found it. They gathered on the bridge, and Dad took forever to find words—he stood in the center, right next to the periscope, his arms extended out a little from his sides, his fingers trilling in the air exactly as Gabriel had done when he first found the salon, as though he could touch everything at once.

"Your model was exactly right," Peter said. They had

all seen the model of the *Nautilus* when the adventure of the Lodgers had taken them down to Nemolab.

Dad laughed. "I didn't actually build that one. I built the rest. I never did really know if it would be exact. But here it is. And I had no idea about…" He stepped over, running his hand along the leather chair backs. "These chair backs, this is whale leather." He looked up.

"I can't believe it," Mom said. "Without you and your crew, this ship never would have been discovered."

Nerissa crouched to look at the periscope. "We've all been focused on the emergency, but I gotta say: This is astonishing."

"Here's what's astonishing," Gabriel said. He let the golden pin drop onto the sonar station with a clang. It rolled to a stop. "Not only did the crew of the *Nautilus* make this ship disappear, but they themselves disappeared without a trace—except for Mickey Land's journal. And I can't guarantee he made it all the way to Antarctica. When Misty and I got here, we expected to find a ship full of skeletons, but they're not here. And they left this clue." He pointed at the message, ALL HANDS TO THE TIGERS. "Engraving it on the pin meant that the clue would be seen by whoever found the *Nautilus* and freed it. They wanted to be found."

Nerissa went over and picked it up, studying it. "The tigers."

Dad put his hands on his hips. "That could be so many things."

289

"Some more than others," Peter said. "We'll figure it out."

"That is if you want to figure it out, Dr. Nemo," Misty said. "Do you want us to work on this?"

"Right." Gabriel nodded at Misty. "Do you want us to discover what really happened to Captain Nemo?"

"Mm," Mom said. "Sometimes people disappear for a reason. But yes. *I* want to know."

"Me too," Dad said.

"We have a project!" Gabriel said, clapping his hands together.

"You have another one first," Dad said.

"What's that?" Misty asked.

"You're gonna need a new ship."

All of them rocked a little when he said this, but Peter recovered first. "We've been working on some ideas..."

But Gabriel shook his head. "Not yet." He wasn't ready. Not for a new *Obscure*.

But that was okay. Right now he had the *Nautilus*.

"Okay," Nerissa said finally. "If this thing was anchored, there has to be a chain we can attach to."

"Attach to?" Gabriel asked.

"For towing," she said. "And this is a big ship, so I have a feeling it's gonna be a slow trip."

"No need," Gabriel said. He grinned as he went to the station that said MAIN POWER. He shifted the switch over, and the *Nautilus* began to thrum. "We have full power."

Dad laughed. "Of course, of course. That was how you got it out of the cave."

Misty was already sliding into the sonar seat. "Sonar active," she said. "Dr. Nemo, if there's a station you'd like to take, you're welcome."

"No ...," Dad said. He put his arm around Mom. "I want to take it all in."

"Engines online," Peter said. "You guys want to see what this thing can do?"

"Where would you like to go?" Gabriel asked, smiling wide. "Hawaii?"

"That's like a couple hundred hours," Peter said. "And I think school would tell us we don't have a couple hundred hours unless we're using them to get home. Right?"

Mom nodded with a smile. "I think it's time to get back."

Gabriel laughed. "California, then. Dad?"

Dad was looking at the periscope in something like reverential wonder when he seemed to come awake. "Hm?"

"Would you like to give the order?"

"Oh." Dad's eyes glistened. "Um. Take us out."

The vast ship began to rumble and then calm and move.

And once more the mighty *Nautilus* took to the sea.

ACKNOWLEDGMENTS

Here we are at the end of another Young Captain Nemo adventure. I can't begin to explain what an honor it has been to explore the depths again and get to know these characters a little more. These books are a reflection of the kind of thing I have always loved to read—a little adventure, a little science fiction. I want to write them so that when you're reading, you can just follow the story, or you can stop to look something up and go: *Huh! That really exists.* So of course I need to tell you: Some of the things in this book don't exist. The geography of Antarctica is a mere shadow of its real self, and while the Weddell Sea exists, there is no Gilbert Trench. But the Gilbert Islands, part of what is now called Kiribati, are really there. And Ned Land really was a character in Jules Verne's *Twenty Thousand Leagues Under the*

Sea, though there was no mention of Mickey. Also if there are really massive cousins of the moray eels under the ice at the bottom of the world, I don't want to meet them, but right now it's a guess. I am also not really sure how to break into a submarine, and if you know, don't tell me. Assembling a book is not one man's accomplishment—to put this book together took grueling hours from my editor, Holly West, and some extraordinarily patient copy editors (Hayley Jozwiak and Josh Berlowitz). I am so indebted to them. Also I can't believe I'm lucky enough to have the help of the people who make these books look as marvelous as they do: art director Katie Klimowicz and artist Eric Hibbeler, whose paintings you see on the covers. I also have to thank my agent, Moe Ferrara, who never runs out of patience.

Finally I have to thank Julia, Julia Sophia, and Katarina— you guys are the ones who have to hear me rehashing plots as I pace around the house, and I love you for inspiring me to get down to writing it.

See you all soon,
Jason Henderson

Thank you for reading this Feiwel & Friends book.

The friends who made **THE QUEST FOR THE NAUTILUS** possible are:

JEAN FEIWEL PUBLISHER

LIZ SZABLA ASSOCIATE PUBLISHER

RICH DEAS SENIOR CREATIVE DIRECTOR

HOLLY WEST SENIOR EDITOR

ANNA ROBERTO SENIOR EDITOR

KAT BRZOZOWSKI SENIOR EDITOR

EMILY SETTLE ASSOCIATE EDITOR

ERIN SIU ASSOCIATE EDITOR

ALEXEI ESIKOFF SENIOR MANAGING EDITOR

KIM WAYMER SENIOR PRODUCTION MANAGER

KATIE KLIMOWICZ SENIOR DESIGNER

HAYLEY JOZWIAK MANAGING EDITOR

FOYINSI ADEGBONMIRE EDITORIAL ASSISTANT

RACHEL DIEBEL ASSISTANT EDITOR

Follow us on Facebook or visit us online at mackids.com

OUR BOOKS ARE FRIENDS FOR LIFE